The Earl's Christmas Pearl

By Megan Frampton

The Hazards of Dukes

Never Kiss a Duke

The Duke's Daughters

The Earl's Christmas Pearl (novella)

Never a Bride

The Lady Is Daring

Lady Be Reckless

Lady Be Bad

Dukes Behaving Badly

My Fair Duchess

Why Do Dukes Fall in Love?

One-Eyed Dukes Are Wild

No Groom at the Inn (novella)

Put Up Your Duke

When Good Earls Go Bad (novella)

The Duke's Guide to Correct Behavior

The Earl's Christmas Pearl

A Duke's Daughters Novella

Megan Frampton

AVONIMPULSE
An Imprint of HarperCollins*Publishers*

Digital Edition OCTOBER 2019 ISBN: 978-0-06-293184-9

Print Edition ISBN: 978-0-06-293185-6

Cover design by Amy Halperin

Cover illustrations by Gregg Gulbronson

FIRST EDITION

19 20 21 22 23 HDC 10 9 8 7 6 5 4 3 2 1

To Gunnar, my dear friend Myretta's departed Welsh Corgi.
You are the inspiration for Mr. Shorty,
and I am grateful for the time you got to spend with Myretta.
Bark on, dude.

Chapter One

On the first day of Christmas,
my true love gave to me
An earl who was very grumpy

"Alone!" Pearl exulted, unable to resist twirling in the hallway of her parents' London town house.

Pearl's first thought, on realizing she'd been left behind, was to dash after the carriage.

Her second thought was definitely not to.

Her third thought was most *definitely* not to.

Which was why she was both exulting and twirling.

Her mother, the Duchess of Marymount, had insisted on driving up from the country for some Christmas shopping. And insisted that Pearl accompany her. Not only because Pearl was the quiet organization behind her mother's chaos, but also because there was an infinitesimal chance that there would be some unsuspecting gentleman who discovered he'd bought a bride along with his Christmas gifts, and the duchess was going to ensure that Pearl was the one he bought.

Even though Pearl did not wish for that at all, something

she'd tried—unsuccessfully—to tell her mother since she'd become the focus of her mother's marital determination.

But even if Pearl, the sole remaining unmarried Howlett sister, had to come with her, she didn't have to go *back* with her. Not if she was accidentally left behind.

The duchess was scattered at the best of times—hence the need for Pearl's steady hand—and under the duress of choosing the right gifts for all her daughters and their husbands and their children—well, small wonder that the duchess ensured everything was properly packed into the carriage.

Except for Pearl.

It might take a few hours, or if Pearl was lucky, a day or two before anyone realized the mistake.

But meanwhile, Pearl was alone. In London. Right before Christmas.

"Alone," she whispered again.

The housekeeper and butler, both of whom resided in the town house when the family was away, had left to spend Christmas with their families, and wouldn't be back until after New Year's Day.

She'd not been alone since—well, *ever*. She had four sisters, after all, including her twin, Olivia. When her sisters had been away, there had always been a maid or a governess or someone to keep company with her—since it was apparently the Worst Thing Ever for a young unmarried lady to be alone.

Except it was the Best Thing Ever.

What should she do first?

She could strap on her skates and try gliding down the hallways. Except she was wobbly on them, and she didn't want to ruin her newfound freedom by breaking a bone or anything.

She could go jump on the beds, something that was most definitely frowned upon by a young lady with certain expectations. But that would disturb the bedding, and she didn't want to make more work for the housekeeper when she returned.

She wanted to be alone, but she wasn't a *monster.*

She could see how long it would take to run from the front door to the uppermost attic. Pearl never got enough physical activity; a young lady was supposed to sit and look placid, two things Pearl was most definitely not good at.

She was always restless, always yearned for some sort of exercise. Something that would make her warm, and perhaps even perspire.

Even though ladies never admitted to perspiring.

She twirled again, spreading her arms out wide, feeling her skirts billow out. If her mother saw her she would be appalled.

Which was the point of doing it, wasn't it?

Her mother wasn't here.

Nobody was here.

She was completely, entirely, and absolutely alone.

She flung her head back and laughed, a joyous laugh that was most definitely not ladylike. It was too loud, too happy, too noticeable.

Just once, Pearl wanted to be loud, happy, and most importantly, *noticeable.*

It was difficult to be the *not* sister—she was not Della, the scandalous runaway eldest sister; she was not Eleanor, the good sister; nor was she her twin Olivia, the very opinionated sister. She was definitely not Ida, who was determined to show everyone how intelligent she was.

She was Pearl. Not any one of the duke's other daughters.

Just once she wanted to be known for who she *was*, not who she was *not*.

"Ooh," she said as the idea popped into her head. Instead of skating, jumping, or running, she would go out and walk *by herself*. Perhaps get a cup of chocolate at a tea shop. Maybe—if she was feeling particularly daring, which she absolutely was—visit a pub and have a glass of ale.

Apparently the consumption of beverages was high on her list of things to do when she was alone.

She strode determinedly toward the front door, then halted when she realized she didn't have a cloak.

It was December, after all, and she'd feel like an idiot if she squandered her precious freedom by getting a cold. And if she got sick she might be the not alive sister, which was definitely *not* the type she wished to be.

"Where could it be?" she mused. She'd never had to think about where her cloak might be; a footman or the butler just appeared with it whenever she went out.

Being alone also meant being responsible for one's self.

Discovering, for example, where outer garments might be stored. She would gladly accept that responsibility; she was an adult female of twenty years, after all—she should have an idea of where clothing was kept, for goodness' sake.

She pivoted to walk toward the back stairs that led to where the servants did their work.

She would locate her cloak, she would put it on without assistance, and she would walk outside without accompaniment.

It was ridiculous how exhilarating those mundane tasks felt.

She found her cloak, eventually, after poking through several cupboards that yielded surprising items such as a porcelain statue of a particularly gruesome-looking shepherdess, a container full of gentlemen's snuffboxes, and several pairs of children's rain boots, likely hers and her sisters' that they had outgrown.

She made a face at the shepherdess, opened one of the snuffboxes and immediately sneezed, and made a mental note to collect the rain boots to send to the Society for Poor and Unfortunate Children.

Once properly dressed for the weather, and collecting the money she hadn't spent on gifts, she opened the door and stepped outside, a huge grin on her face. She'd never opened the front door to the town house herself, and it felt wonderful to do so, even more so when it was just her in the open air.

It was drizzling, one of those half-hearted storms that punctuated winter in London. But for Pearl, it felt as though the sun was blazing.

She skipped down the stairs, holding her arms out for balance, slid on the final step, which was damp from the rain, and wobbled onto the sidewalk, her heart racing from the near accident.

She was righting herself when she felt a hand clamp onto her arm.

"Do you need some help?" a man's voice said, sounding entirely displeased he'd had to ask. He spoke in some sort of accent, but Pearl couldn't place it.

"No, thank you," Pearl replied, straightening as she shook the man's arm off. It was rude, but then again it was rude to hold on to another person in the first place. Especially when one did not need assistance.

"Good." The man's tone was even more curt, and Pearl felt a rebuke welling up inside her—something she normally resisted, what with being a lady and all—but now, on her own, alone, she would do as she pleased.

"I am perfectly capable of . . . " she began, raising her eyes to him.

Oh.

His expression was indeed fearsome—the gruesome shepherdess might even cede the field of unpleasant expressions to him—but the scowl was on one of the most compelling faces she'd ever seen.

He had dark hair, nearly black, and his eyes were dark as well, surrounded by dark, thick lashes. His eyebrows were two strong slashes, and his nose was an equally sharp blade. His cheekbones were prominent, and he had stubble on his cheeks, indicating it had been some time since he'd shaved.

He looked like the physical manifestation of all the brooding heroes in the shocking novels Olivia loved. And that Pearl secretly read as well.

Pearl felt a whoosh in her stomach and knew it was a visceral reaction to him.

An equally strong reaction happened when she spotted the little dog winding around the man's long legs. It was light brown, with ears that almost seemed too big for its body, and its face appeared to be smiling.

"Oh," she said, beginning to bend down to scratch the dog's head. She leapt back up when the man tugged on the leash, jerking the dog away from her hand. The dog seemed to frown because of being denied the opportunity to receive petting, but Pearl might have been reading into that.

"I'll be off then, since you don't need me," the man said, giving a brief nod. "Come on, Mr. Shorty." He and his dog walked down the sidewalk, the dog glancing back to look at her.

She stared at him for another moment—that whooshing feeling still unsettling her stomach—then set off down the street in the opposite direction, resolving to look as though she had a purpose and wasn't just wandering around the city searching for beverages. And definitely not as though she were a young lady tasting her first draught of freedom.

And—"Mr. Shorty?" she said aloud, chuckling.

She glanced back in his direction, surprised to see him walking up the steps to Lady Robinson's house. Hm. Lady Robinson lived alone.

What was he doing there?

Owen cursed himself as he walked slowly up the stairs to his godmother's town house. He hadn't been able to resist reaching out to steady the woman, even though he did not want to converse with anyone at all, either now or in the future.

He wanted to be alone.

Alone to recover from his injury, alone to ponder how he would deal with his mother and sisters' determination to marry him off, and alone to concentrate on his business interests.

Alone without being the focus of everyone's attention.

"And there's you, of course," he said to Mr. Shorty, who was having just as hard a time going up the stairs, but his dog's issue was the shortness of his legs, not that his leg was injured. "I'm not truly alone, am I, if you're with me?"

Mr. Shorty did not reply.

Owen shrugged, then swung the door open, limping inside. Mr. Shorty trotted off toward the kitchen, knowing a treat was in the offing. His godmother's housekeeper had remained to take care of Owen while he was in town, and she'd learned to stay out of his way, even as she cultivated Mr. Shorty's acquaintance.

But even she would be leaving in a day or two, going to spend Christmas with her family.

Owen slowly removed his cloak, wincing at the pain in his shoulder. His right-hand man, Enfys, had offered to come to London to valet for him, but Owen had refused. Christmas was in a few days, and Enfys should be with his family, not fussing over Owen.

He hadn't always been so grouchy; at one point in his life he'd been almost cheerful. *Almost.*

But then he'd inherited his father's title as well as the mess his father had created. And the care and feeding of his three sisters, plus his mother, who alternated between insisting she could take care of herself and then complaining when things didn't go as precisely as she'd hoped.

He walked down the hall to the library, where he was conducting his business. He found it comforting to be surrounded by books, inanimate objects that could reveal knowledge if he looked hard enough.

Unfortunately he hadn't consulted a book about the danger of groundhogs until it was too late.

He'd been helping to shear the sheep on the farm when his foot twisted in a groundhog hole, and he'd fallen, injuring both his leg and shoulder.

If he were being honest with himself, he had to admit it was a relief to have to come to London to recuperate, especially at Christmas, with so much focus on the family. It was when they were all together that the crescendo of pleas for him to marry was the highest. As though his family wouldn't immediately find fault with whatever woman he chose.

But that wasn't fair, was it? His family loved him and they wanted him to be happy; they just didn't understand him. Or, perhaps more accurately, they understood only that his purpose in their lives was to assist them. The few times he'd asked for help from his family he'd been met with blank stares. He knew it was because they saw him as set up on a pedestal to be admired, not assisted. Eventually he hoped to find someone who saw him as a man, faults and all. And if that person were female? He'd leap off his pedestal so quickly to embrace her he'd likely break something else in his leg.

Until that happened, however, at least he had Mr. Shorty, who was most appreciative of whatever Owen did for him, showing his thanks with barks and slobber.

That young lady hadn't thanked him, had she? If anything, she had nearly growled at him when he'd offered his help.

Perhaps she was his perfect match? He chuckled at the thought.

He heard a noise and turned to see his godmother's housekeeper standing at the entrance to the library, a surprised expression on her face. Because he was smiling and laughing?

"My lord?"

I do smile sometimes, you know, he wanted to say.

"Yes, Mrs. Hopkins?"

"If it's all right with you, I'll be leaving after supper. My sister wrote and said that—"

"Fine, fine," Owen interrupted, waving his hand in dismissal.

"Fine," Mrs. Hopkins repeated, sounding stiff. She turned on her heel and walked back toward the kitchen.

Had he managed to offend her? He'd spoken five words, at most. He certainly had a talent for it.

Damn it, he wished he could figure out these kind of small interactions better—he never knew when he was about to make an ass of himself. Or horribly offend someone when he didn't intend to.

"Thank you, Mrs. Hopkins," he called in what he hoped was a grateful tone after the housekeeper's retreating figure.

Nine words. Hopefully those last four hadn't also offended her.

Owen shrugged as he surveyed the papers he'd been working on prior to taking his doctor-mandated walk. It wasn't as though he could do anything about his personality. Thirty years of being precisely like himself could tell him that much.

What he could, and would, do, is focus on regaining his strength, tending to his business, and relishing being alone.

"Sounds bleak, Owen," he murmured with a rueful shake of his head.

Mr. Shorty trotted back into the office, flopping down on the pillows Owen had snagged for a dog bed.

"At least I have you," Owen said, lowering his hand to pat Mr. Shorty's head.

Chapter Two

On the second day of Christmas
my true love gave to me
Two sharp knocks on the
door demanding entry

Pearl wasn't feeling *quite* as adventurous as she trudged home to her parents' house.

For one thing, the hot cocoa had not been very good. It had lumps, and when Pearl had pointed that out to the server, she had been told in no uncertain terms that there was nothing to be done about it. The server had then bustled away to help other customers before Pearl could even utter a retort. Especially galling, since she had been thinking about replying "So I can lump it and leave?"

The server would never hear her brilliance.

She'd left the café, giving a moderate tip, and then had peeked in at a nearby pub, but the clientele looked far too male for her to venture inside.

Was there a pub for ladies, or was that just called a drawing room?

And the drizzling rain, which had kept up while she was inside the café, was now a downpour, sending icy raindrops to the back of her neck and down her cloak. She had looked in vain for a cab, but there were none to be had.

Not that she knew how to hail one, but she wouldn't even get the opportunity to try.

Perhaps being alone was not so wonderful after all.

She perked up, however, when she turned onto her street. Soon she'd be home, and she'd be able to find something to eat.

The house still looked empty, so the duchess still hadn't realized Pearl had been left behind.

"More time to be alone," Pearl whispered to herself. That was good, wasn't it?

The stairs were even more slippery when she walked up, and she glanced over at Lady Robinson's house, the one she'd seen the gruff, handsome gentleman enter.

Lady Robinson was not the friendliest neighbor. So perhaps this man was an equally distant relative? Was there a proviso in the family charter that all of them had to be abrupt?

She grinned at the thought.

Pearl would have liked to pet the dog, who seemed friendly, at least. She chuckled again at "Mr. Shorty." The dog's owner couldn't be all bad; he had a dog, and his dog had such a funny name.

She would give him the benefit of the doubt. If she ever saw him again, that is. She rather hoped she would, if only so she could appraise his overabundance of masculine beauty.

Damn that whooshing stomach of hers.

Or perhaps she was just hungry?

She stepped inside the house, removing her cloak and spreading it out on the floor so it could dry.

No one was there, either to move the cloak to a more suitable place or to chide her about leaving it on the floor.

"Stay," she commanded the garment, laughing as she spoke. She glanced down at her sodden feet. She could just take her shoes off, couldn't she? Nobody was here to be scandalized.

Determined, she plopped down on the floor to remove them. Her wet stockings slid a little bit on the parquet floor when she stood up, and she stuck her hands out for balance.

It was nearly like skating, only without as much danger of breaking a bone. Hm. She tested her balance, then pushed off on one stockinged foot, trying to glide across the floor, laughing as she stumbled.

A bit of practice, and soon she was sliding with ease, her arms held out parallel to the floor. She hummed a tune as she went, almost as though she were on stage.

Her mother would be scandalized. Which was precisely the point of doing it.

She already felt better, the hot chocolate incident merely a hiccup in her adventure. Now to find some food, she decided. It had to be similar to finding her cloak. She walked toward the kitchen and descended the stairs, wishing she had a candle or something to light the way.

It was awfully dark.

After a half hour of searching, stumbling over pots and stools and all sorts of things she couldn't see, Pearl had to acknowledge defeat.

She was cold and she was hungry, and she had no idea how to solve either problem.

The servants had done an excellent job of closing up the house for Christmas—not a scrap of food anywhere, except for big bags of flour and sugar.

She didn't think she could subsist on that. Especially since she had never cooked anything in her life before. There were servants for that.

Unless there were not.

Drat. Unless the duchess suddenly rolled up in her carriage holding a roast beef in her lap, she would have to figure something out. And then also figure out how to keep herself warm.

She felt her mouth twist and her stomach whoosh as she realized what she was going to have to do. He had offered his help earlier, out on the sidewalk. She hadn't needed it then, but she'd have to take him up on it now.

Owen scowled even more than usual when he heard the knock on the door. Mrs. Hopkins had left right after serving his dinner, and he and Mr. Shorty were sitting in front of the fireplace in the library, Owen with a brandy and Mr. Shorty with a bone. The room was cozy, and Owen felt relief that it wouldn't be possible for him to offend any of the present company.

He was tempted to ignore the knock, and nearly did, but then the person knocked again.

Likely they could see the light of the candle from the front step.

"Hold on," Owen called out, getting up from his chair. His leg ached from his walk earlier, and he had to steady himself to reach a full standing position.

The knock came again, more impatiently, if it were possible for a knock to be impatient.

Which, Owen decided as he limped down the hallway, it was.

"What do you want?" he barked as he opened the door.

The lady blinked at him, her mouth open in surprise. Why was *she* surprised when she had been the one knocking?

"Uh . . ." she began, pulling the hood of her cloak down, "I know Lady Robinson is not in residence, unless she has returned—?" Her tone was hopeful.

"I regret she has not."

She twisted her mouth in disappointment. "Is it possible for me to come in anyway? I have a pressing issue."

It was the lady from next door. He couldn't very well deny her pressing issue. He was a budding misanthrope, but he wasn't *that* miserable.

Besides, something about her intrigued him. Perhaps because she was clearly a young lady who didn't have any of the usual accoutrements young ladies usually did? Things like a chaperone, a lady's maid, or an annoying giggle?

"Come in then," he said, holding the door open wider. She slipped inside, and he shut the door, suddenly keenly aware that she was a young lady. And he, purportedly, was a gentleman.

And they were alone in an empty house.

This was entirely inappropriate.

He'd have to let her know; it was the right thing to do.

"I cannot allow you to stay," he said, watching as her face fell. "I am here alone, and you are a young lady. I would not wish for anything—for anybody to think things." He frowned. "You don't have a chaperone or lady's maid or anything?"

"If I did, don't you think I would have brought her?"

She had a point.

"In which case, I have to repeat my previous statement. It is inappropriate for us to be alone in this house."

She bit her lip as she regarded him for a long moment. "I appreciate your concern. But nobody would know it was inappropriate if they didn't know in the first place, would they?"

He considered her words and the possible consequences.

"I don't wish to marry you," she added hastily. "I can promise you that I will take all the blame if anyone finds out."

She was determined, and he needed to find out what was so pressing so he could help her. If he didn't help, he would be tormented by the knowledge that he hadn't done everything he possibly could—the unfortunate by-product of being the only gentleman in a family of females. His height, his wealth, and his business acumen were in equal demand when he was home in Wales.

He acknowledged her words with a brief dip of his head. "I assure you that I am a gentleman and will behave . . . appropriately."

"Thank you."

"So what is so pressing you must flout convention and knock on my door?" he asked.

"The thing is," she began, clutching her cloak more tightly around her, "I find that I am hungry, and it appears there is no food in our kitchen."

Owen squinted at her, confused. "But you have a cook, certainly?"

She looked embarrassed, which made Owen even more confused. Could she not afford one? His godmother had told him the neighbors were well-heeled; perhaps this was a poor relation?

But why was she in the house in the first place?

He had more questions about her than he'd literally had about anyone else he had met.

"Look, you'd better come sit down," he said, turning on his heel and walking back toward the library.

He heard her follow, and Mr. Shorty trotted out of the room uttering a few yips of welcome.

"Good dog," she murmured.

His dog could offer a proper reception to a guest, at least.

"Have a seat." He gestured toward the sofa. He dragged his chair from behind the desk and set it far enough to be respectable and yet close enough so he could hear her.

"Can you explain, Miss . . . ?" he said.

"Lady Pearl Howlett," she replied. "And you are?"

"Owen Dwyfor, Earl of Llanover. A pleasure to make your acquaintance."

She gave a wry smile. "Is it?"

"Uh—" he began, only to stop speaking when she waved her hand. It was unnerving to encounter someone so blunt. He liked it, to be honest.

"Never mind," she replied. "To answer your question, there is no cook in the house. No housekeeper, no butler, not even a scullery maid. I am completely and entirely alone." Instead of sounding anxious, as one would expect from a gently born lady in the situation, she sounded nearly gleeful.

A lady after his own heart, perhaps? But a lady who was also hungry.

"Let's go to the kitchen," Owen said, getting up as he spoke. He grabbed one of the candles from the table and strode ahead. "Come along, Mr. Shorty," he added.

The lady hopped up from her seat and followed him, Mr. Shorty trotting after.

An earl. And a Welsh earl, if she wasn't mistaken. She'd finally placed his accent, plus his name was Owen. And he owned a Welsh corgi.

How much more Welsh could he be?

"Why are you in Lady Robinson's town house, by the way?" she asked as he guided her to the kitchen.

"She's my godmother," he said abruptly. As it seemed he said most things.

"Ah. But why are you here and she is not?" Pearl continued.

She smothered a chuckle as she heard him growl. She'd think he really was a grump if she hadn't heard how his voice softened when he called his dog. Or how concerned he'd looked when she'd said she needed help.

"My godmother is visiting family."

That was not an answer.

She was opening her mouth to speak again when he continued. "I am in London to consult with doctors." He gestured to his leg. "I've got an injury the doctor at home believed would be better cared for here."

Ah, she hadn't taken notice before, but now he'd said it, she saw he did have a definite limp. She'd been too busy cataloging how attractive he was to notice.

"How did it happen?"

She heard him utter a noise of frustration.

"You know," she said in a matter-of-fact tone, "it is a good thing it wasn't my sister Olivia who got stranded here. Olivia is my twin, and she is the most inquisitive person. Olivia would be demanding all the particulars of your injury, your provenance, and why you are so determined not to share anything. *I* am merely making conversation."

"I guess I should be grateful," he said in a voice that nearly sounded amused.

Perhaps she would be able to befriend him after all?

Because being alone was wonderful, she assured herself. But it wasn't nearly as much fun as teasing a handsome grumpy Welsh gentleman.

"The kitchen is through here," he said, leading them through a narrow hallway. His body appeared to take up all the available space, and she felt that whooshing feeling again.

It's just hunger, she told herself firmly.

They entered the kitchen. After he'd set his candle down and lit some of the lamps, she could see it was spotlessly tidy, with pots and pans hanging up on hooks from the ceiling. A large cupboard stood on the right-hand side, bowls and other dishware visible through the glass of the doors. Her gaze lit on a half-eaten round of cheese and some bread on a wooden board.

She knew she made some sort of sound, but she couldn't help herself. Food! That she didn't need to know how to cook!

"Help yourself," the earl said, gesturing to the board. "I can hear you're famished."

She'd be embarrassed if she weren't starving.

Pearl cut off a big hunk of cheese and tore a bit of bread from the loaf. And then froze. She wasn't sure what protocol she should follow, this situation not having been covered by any etiquette guide: *How to Fend Off Hunger While Also Maintaining Proper Deportment. And Did We Mention You Would Be Alone with a Large Welsh Earl?* Did she stay and gobble everything up here? Should she wrap it in something and take it back to her house?

"If you want to eat it here, that's fine," he said gruffly, as though reading her mind. Or her nonexistent etiquette guide. "Or you could take it back to your house."

Suddenly she didn't want to return to her house. Even though it meant spending more time with the taciturn earl. Or because it meant spending more time with him?

Pearl knew she liked to solve puzzles, but she hadn't anticipated wanting to solve a puzzle like him. And yet here she was, intensely curious.

Of course, the one thing she and all her sisters had in common was an abiding curiosity. So at least she was being consistent.

Perhaps that was their family's charter. Constant curiosity.

"Would you mind sitting with me?" she said as she hoisted herself up onto a wooden stool.

He paused, and she wondered if he was going to just say no and walk out, when he surprised her by sitting down, reaching for the cheese, and slicing a piece off.

"I don't like to eat alone," Pearl said before taking a bite of the cheese. It was some type of cheddar, but it could have been sawdust cheese for all she cared. "Not that I've ever eaten alone, but when I thought about it, I just knew it wouldn't be nearly as nice as eating with someone else." She turned and looked at him. His gaze was intense, and that whole whooshing feeling returned. "You are going to eat something, aren't you? Because otherwise I'm just here eating your food and you're just sitting here watching me."

"I'm not watching you," he replied, popping his bite of cheese into his mouth. As he watched her.

Pearl rolled her eyes. Discreetly, but she rolled them nonetheless. Likely he was regarding her so intently because he was counting down the minutes until she appeared ready to leave.

That thought made her chew more slowly. And keep her gaze on him.

Chapter Three

On the third day of Christmas,
my true love gave to me
Three pieces of cheddar cheese

His unexpected guest was unexpected in other ways also, Owen thought. For one thing, she was not at all what he'd expected a young well-born English lady to be like; she was curious and confident and appeared to have her own opinions about things.

For another thing, she was pretty in such an intriguing way he found it nearly impossible to look away from her. Especially her mouth; it was wide and seemed always on the verge of breaking into a big smile. As though she were planning mischief, and she wanted someone to join her.

Her eyes were a soft brown, nearly the color of his Balwen sheep. Her hair was lighter than her eyes, the color of sheep's wool when it hadn't been washed for some time.

Not that he thought she hadn't washed her hair.

Damn it, now even his talking to himself was resulting in offense.

"How did you injure yourself?" she asked before he'd have to resort to calling himself out for his own infraction. Which would be awkward, since he was already injured.

"Uh—" he began, the sting of embarrassment slowing his reply.

"It's just us here, and I'm eating, so you have to do the talking," she pointed out before taking another big bite of cheese. He liked that she wasn't taking dainty lady bites. But that did mean she was going to be a long time chewing.

The alternative to not talking was sitting in silence while she ate, which seemed as though it was the less preferable option.

Even though that remained to be seen, depending on what he ended up saying.

"I am a sheep farmer in Wales," he began, waiting for her expression to change to one of disdain. Instead, she only looked more curious, making a hand motion for him to continue.

"And I was shearing sheep when I stepped in a hole. Likely made by a groundhog." Owen loathed groundhogs. At least now. "I fell, and I didn't want to fall on the sheep, so I twisted and hit my shoulder and did something to my leg. I didn't break it, but it is difficult to walk."

"You probably strained a muscle," she replied. "I did that once when I was playing cricket."

Owen's eyes widened. This lady played cricket? She was most definitely not like any lady he'd met before.

Not that he'd met that many, something his sisters and mother frequently pointed out.

"Go on," she urged.

"There's not much more to say," Owen said, feeling sheepish. So to speak.

"What did the doctor say? Are you being treated? I didn't see you with a cane this morning. Are you supposed to be using one?"

Ah. So there *was* more to say.

"I'm being treated, yes, for a few more weeks. Until after Christmas, I believe." She immediately looked upset, and he hastened to reassure her.

Not something he'd ever done before.

"Christmas isn't that important to me," he said. *Too much family, too many people, too much importance placed on the right thing to say, do, or give.*

"Not important?" she sputtered. "But it's Christmas!" As though that was the answer, even though he had just acknowledged that it was, indeed, Christmas.

"We agree on that," he replied, chuckling at her outraged expression. "Why are you here by yourself anyway? No family, no servants, no food! After all, it's nearly Christmas!" he exclaimed, widening his eyes and waggling his brows in mock horror.

She grinned as she poked him in the shoulder. And then her expression changed to one of panic. "I didn't just touch your injury, did I? Oh my goodness, I am so sorry."

"It's the other shoulder. It's fine," he said in what he hoped was a reassuring manner.

"Thank goodness," she said, relieved. "I wouldn't want to be responsible for exacerbating your injury while taking advantage of your hospitality."

"As to your questions," he replied, surprised that he actually wanted to answer them, "I do have a cane, and I am supposed to walk slowly for at least an hour a day. I see the doctor again after Christmas, and then if he is satisfied with my progress, I can return home."

She nodded, a thoughtful expression on her face. "I think that is what I did after my injury. It must hurt a great deal."

"Uh—yes." He realized he didn't quite know how to respond to her sincerity. "I mean, it's getting better. It does get sore after I walk." His family had expressed sympathy, but had quickly followed up their words with concern for what he wouldn't be able to do for them until after he'd fully recovered. She made no such caveat. Her sympathy was without any strings of commitment.

"Well, I am glad you are improving."

There was a moment of silence, during which his mind scrambled to find something to say. Thankfully, she began speaking before he could blurt anything else out.

"I am full, thank you," she said, putting her hand on her belly. "I should go. I know you didn't anticipate having a guest." She hopped off the stool and he hastened to stand also.

"I can see you out," he said.

She shook her head decisively, making her hair tumble around her face. He didn't think he had ever met such a decided woman. "I know the way, thank you."

"Would you want to come by tomorrow morning? For breakfast?" he asked before he realized he was even speaking.

She froze, giving him a bemused stare. No wonder, given

that he'd been gruff and awkward. "Well, yes. That is very generous of you, my lord."

"Owen," he replied. Even though he knew that a young English lady would be horrified to call such a recent acquaintance by his given name. But this was a completely unusual circumstance, and he couldn't see "my lord" and "my ladying" one another when they were together alone. That would make it even more awkward.

She smiled. Not horrified then. "Owen. And I am Pearl. I will see you tomorrow morning then."

She slipped out of the room, leaving him wondering what the hell he had just done.

Owen. Pearl slid the name around in her mind, then couldn't help but utter it aloud. "Owen." She walked into her house, wishing for the first time it wasn't quite so large.

And cold.

And solitary.

She hadn't thought this whole alone thing through, had she? Being alone meant not only that there was no food, but also that there was no one to stoke the fires. For goodness' sake, she didn't even know what "stoke" meant.

There was no one to even ask what "stoke" meant in the first place.

Perhaps she did want her mother to collect her soon after all. But that would mean not getting to talk to Owen. And pet Mr. Shorty.

So, no. She did not want her mother to come soon. Which meant she had to figure all this out on her own.

"Wood. I need wood," she muttered as she walked into the drawing room. It didn't make sense, as she thought about it, to try to sleep in her own bedroom—she'd need to keep herself centrally located so as to preserve her resources. "And something warm." She already felt chilled, and she hadn't yet taken off her cloak. But she could do this. She *could*. It just meant gathering blankets and building a fire and making sure she didn't burn the house down.

Far easier than, say, walking into a ballroom where everyone knew *of* you but didn't know you. They just knew about your family's scandal, your talkative mother, your laconic father, and that you were "the other one" in relation to any of your sisters.

Burning the house down might be a relief from all that, honestly. At least she'd be warm.

Within an hour, Pearl had gotten the fire sufficiently stoked and was lying in front of it wrapped in the comforters she had dragged from the beds.

It was . . . cozy. She was alone, but she was warm, she had done something for herself, and she had met the large, exceedingly attractive earl.

Not to mention Mr. Shorty, who had licked her hand. Which, she had to say, the exceedingly attractive earl had not.

Which brought to mind all sorts of intriguing scenarios, ones she had never seriously thought about before.

Of course she had noticed attractive men before, but they had usually already been involved with one or another of her sisters. The men she'd met out in Society were interchangeable, always glancing over her head to see who else was at the party, or asking pointed questions about her father's fortune and what her own dowry might be.

The Welsh earl didn't know anything about her or her family. He hadn't met any of her sisters or her parents.

He just knew *her*. That felt as remarkable as being left alone in the town house or managing to start a fire.

Owen wished he had specified a time for the young lady—Pearl—to come over. As it was, he kept glancing out the window to see if she was on his steps yet. He wasn't attending to his business, nor was he performing his exercises as his doctor had instructed.

Mr. Shorty seemed equally on edge, raising his head from his pillow to whimper every so often.

He'd slept wonderfully the night before, something that hadn't happened since his injury—usually he ended up rolling over in his sleep, which made his leg or shoulder hurt, and then he woke up cursing.

Not last night. Last night, he'd slept all the night through, Mr. Shorty curled up in a warm bundle against his back.

Was it because he was finally alone in London? Or was it something—or someone—else?

He did not want to answer his own question.

Likely it was the cheese. That was it, he told himself firmly.

He leapt up when he heard the knock at the door, then grimaced as the pain shot up his leg.

Mr. Shorty rose too, trotting ahead of Owen as Owen limped his way to the door.

"Good morning, Owen," she said in a cheery voice as she stepped inside. Her cheeks were pink from the cold, which he felt as the wind gusted. Owen shut the door hastily, then turned to greet her.

"Good morning, Pearl."

He didn't feel the cold as she turned her bright smile on him. He wondered what it would be like to be in a good mood most of the time. Or was she? Perhaps she wasn't accorded the opportunity to show her grumpiness, like he was.

The benefit of being the head of one's household—they could, and would, complain about his gruffness, but they didn't punish him for it.

He'd need to ask about her family at some point. Given that none of them seemed to be in London right now. And so close to Christmas. As she'd pointed out. Did that mean she would be alone too?

But first he had to feed her. "We have some bread and eggs, if you want to come to the kitchen."

"Eggs?" she said in a pleased tone. "Is your cook here? I do love eggs." He marveled at her ability to demonstrate enthusiasm for the most basic things, like cheese and eggs.

Owen chuckled as he led the way back down to the kitchen. "No, I am going to cook them myself."

He heard a startled noise behind him and shook his head in mock disapproval. "Do you mean to tell me, Lady Pearl, that you have never cooked an egg?"

She snorted, at which he suppressed a laugh. He didn't know if ladies liked to be caught snorting.

"Of course not." They entered the kitchen, and she took the stool she'd sat on the night before while he went to take the eggs out of the larder. "I can dance, I can embroider, I can speak passable French, provided you want to know how I take my tea, and I can paint, if you want pictures of bunnies." She spoke in a dejected tone. "Rabbits, I mean," she corrected.

Owen blinked. "Bunnies?" he said, walking over to the stove with the eggs.

She looked embarrassed. "I haven't really mastered anything else. So I decided to concentrate on the things that made me happy. Like bunnies."

The things that made her happy.

Had Owen ever thought about the things that made him happy before?

He'd certainly spent a fair amount of time considering what made him unhappy—his sisters and mother pestering him to marry, his wool not fetching the price at market he knew it was worth.

Being in London nursing an injury.

Although now that didn't seem quite so bad. The London part, not the injury part. That was still bad.

"How do you like your eggs?" he asked. He did not want to think about his unhappiness list anymore.

She came to stand beside him, peering over his shoulder. "Fried, I suppose. Can you teach me how to do it? How to cook eggs?"

He glanced over his shoulder at her. "Because a young lady of privilege will ever have call to make eggs?"

She wrinkled her nose. "I suppose I won't. But that doesn't mean I shouldn't learn." She folded her arms over her chest. "So teach me."

Owen couldn't help but smile in response to her demanding tone, then frowned as her expression changed to one of shock.

"What is it?"

"Nothing," she replied, shaking her head. "Go ahead, I am listening."

That smile. My goodness, his smile ought to be illegal. He was merely extremely attractive before his mouth widened into a smile; when he smiled, his whole face changed, making his eyes glint with humor and one corner of his mouth curl up higher than the other.

She caught herself before she said something about why she'd reacted so strongly; after all, it wasn't usually proper to blurt something out about how gorgeous another person was, especially if that person was a grumpy Welsh earl who wasn't nearly as grumpy as he seemed at first.

Which made him entirely more dangerous.

"I lit the stove earlier, but usually you'd make certain the stove was on." He held his hand over the top, spreading his fingers. "It feels hot enough. You try."

Pearl extended her hand over the surface, imitating his action. "How hot does it have to be?" she asked.

"You'll see when we put the butter in the pan." He turned to slice a thick pat of butter and dropped it into a skillet on the stove. It immediately began to sizzle, and he grabbed a fork to poke at the butter, which was fast becoming a brown puddle.

"That's a little too hot. You don't want it to melt the butter immediately."

"Ah," Pearl said, even though she had no idea how she would regulate the temperature of the stove. But she didn't want to ask and reveal her entire ignorance of the kitchen. Even though of course he knew she would have no idea of what happened here, being a lady and all.

Still, she didn't want to admit it.

"But it's fine as long as we put the eggs in quickly." He picked an egg up and cracked it with one hand into the skillet.

Pearl's eyes widened. "You have to show me how to do that!" she demanded.

"What, crack an egg?" His smile was wry, as though he was amused that she was so impressed.

Because you're an earl, and a man, for goodness' sake, and yet you can do domestic things like crack eggs!

She didn't think even her handsome brothers-in-law could do that.

"Here, you try." He placed an egg in her hand, then wrapped his hand around hers.

She tried not to make an indication that this was the first time she had touched a gentleman's hand without gloves on. Nor did she want to indicate what the sight of their hands—one over the other—did to her insides.

"So as a beginner you should use two hands." He reached across her and took her other hand, then drew both hands over to a bowl. "We won't cook this one, this is just for practice." His hand was still on hers. "Now tap the egg gently on the edge of the bowl."

She did, feeling the egg crack.

"Now what?" she said in panic, looking up at him.

Oops. *Mistake.* All that handsomeness right in her vision made her forget entirely about what she was doing.

His eyes stared into hers, and it seemed as though he too had forgotten.

"Uh," he began. She saw his cheeks redden. She looked away, back at the egg, which was starting to seep from the inside.

"You separate the shell and drop the egg into the bowl." His voice sounded strained.

She didn't trust herself to speak, so she just nodded and did as he'd said. A few pieces of shell landed in the bowl, and she leaned forward to pick them out.

But she had done it.

"Can I crack the next one into the skillet?" she asked excitedly, looking back up at him again. This time she was more prepared.

Even though her stomach still whooshed. Hunger, yes, but also—hunger of a different sort.

Mistake, mistake, mistake a voice clamored in her head.

Or is it an adventure? another voice asked in a sly tone.

Who needed sisters around when you had a whole Greek chorus in residence in your head?

"Go ahead," he said, placing another egg in her palm.

She tapped it on the edge of the bowl, then swiftly moved it above the skillet, dropping it into the pan. It sizzled, and she grinned.

She had successfully cracked an egg.

And was currently alone with a gentleman who was not only not incredibly grumpy, but who was willing to teach her things.

Hm . . . that second voice said.

Oh dear.

Chapter Four

On the fourth day of Christmas,
my true love gave to me
Four eggs because we were so hungry

Owen had never had so much fun cooking eggs before.

He could almost say he had never had so much fun before, but that would be to deny the moments with his sisters that had brought him happiness—playing hide-and-seek when they were all small and finding one of his sisters, Gwyneth, asleep in a hedge; competing in charades with his most educated sister, Bryn; singing Christmas carols with his entire family except his father, who was most often to be found in his office.

And now it was Owen who was usually in his office. No time for singing or cooking eggs or sharing a smile with a stranger.

He finished cooking his portion, then slid the eggs onto a plate and joined her at the table.

"Mm, these are excellent," she said. She had already eaten one of them. They were small, so he'd made four for each of them. He figured they were both hungry after all. "Thank you," she continued, nodding at him.

"You are welcome. Thank you for the excellent cracking skills. *Cracking* good, I'd say."

And then he froze, because had he just made a terrible pun? Out loud to someone he'd just met?

She grinned, then put her hand over her mouth and began to laugh.

He had.

But at least it seemed she appreciated it? He'd stopped sharing puns aloud with his sisters when all he got in return was groaning and eye rolls.

"You're really getting me to come out of my shell," she said with a wink.

He felt his eyes widen and something inside his chest—was it his heart?—lurch in an odd way.

"Are you yolking with me?" he replied in a mock serious tone.

She rolled her eyes and groaned, only not the aggravated way his sisters did; more as though she very much appreciated his wit and was complimenting him with the most appropriate response.

"I might have to go lay down, your jokes are so hen-witted," she said at last. It was clear she was racking her brain to think of more puns. He felt that thing in his chest respond to that as well.

"No need to crow about it," he shot back.

She shook her head. "I acknowledge defeat." Her eyes sparkled. "But instead of being *cooped up* here, how about we go out and ruffle some feathers?"

"Go out?" he said in surprise.

Her face fell, and he wished he could take his words back. *Of course I want to go outside with you. I'm just surprised you suggested it.*

"If you don't wish to, that is fine," she said in a stiff tone of voice. "I just thought that since your dog needs walking, and you mentioned you needed to walk, and I am feeling restless that you might—"

He nodded before she had finished speaking. "Of course. Mr. Shorty does need a walk. A perfect suggestion. I was just startled."

Startled by how he felt right now. How she was making him feel.

Her expression eased, and that constricted feeling in his chest loosened.

"We should purchase some decorations for Christmas," she said in a decided tone. "Since you'll be here."

It was on the tip of his tongue to ask—*will you be here too?*—only he didn't want to make her nervous about his presence. And besides, she was still speaking.

"I presume you have a feather to fly with for some purchases?" she added in a sly tone.

"Plucked from the labors of my sheep, thank you very much," he said, feeling how he was actually grinning back at her.

She laughed and poked him in the arm.

"I'll return in a few moments, I just have to gather my things," she said as she left the kitchen. "I'll meet you and Mr. Shorty outside in five minutes?"

"I'll be walking on eggshells until you arrive," he replied.

Pearl couldn't stop smiling as she went from his house to hers. The very grumpy earl was much less grumpy when he allowed himself to interact with someone.

And she liked that he had allowed himself to interact with her.

She didn't feel lonely any longer; instead, she felt a heightened sense of excitement, of anticipation. As though this was a wonderful Christmas dream that she would have to wake from eventually, but was lovely while she was sleeping.

She bit her lip as she entered the house, glancing around in case her mother had tracked her down. And wondered at how relieved she was when the house remained empty—she called out, but her voice just echoed in the hallway.

In a few minutes, she was back outside, her money put safely in her pocket, her cloak wrapped around her against the cold.

The sky looked dark, even though it was only midmorning, and it seemed as though she could smell the weather about to change. It was crisply cold, and she exhaled, watching her breath hang in the air.

But she was warm, not just from her cloak, but from the filling breakfast, the comradery, and the feeling that she'd discovered a secret, hidden part of him that he didn't allow people to see—the part that made puns, and eggs, with an equal bashful pride.

It was ridiculously charming in a gentleman as ruggedly and thoroughly handsome as he.

She watched as he exited his house, closing the door

carefully behind him, allowing Mr. Shorty to go ahead down the stairs as he made his way behind him, grimacing from the pain every so often.

"Here, let me help." She ran up the stairs and took his arm without waiting for his reply. She felt him stiffen, but then he gave a brief nod, and they descended the rest of the way in silence, her feeling his much greater weight against her.

"I hope you have an idea of where we should go," he said gruffly as he let go of her arm. She immediately took it again, looking up at him with an "I dare you" expression on her face.

He frowned, but didn't shake her off.

"Of course I do," she replied confidently, even though the range of her shopping knowledge was limited to stores that sold toys or jewelry.

As it turned out, Pearl was good at faking knowledge she didn't have, a skill she hadn't known she possessed until now. She led the earl to Regent Street, and then to some of the streets that ran alongside it, where aspiring merchants were hoping to catch the eye of the most wealthy shoppers.

"Oh, we need to get some of this," Pearl said as she spied a cart heaped with holly. The man in charge spotted them immediately and walked forward, an eager look on his face.

"My holly is the best, my lord, my lady. Sure to decorate your home as prettily as anything you'll find."

"We're not—" the earl began.

Pearl elbowed him, and he stopped speaking.

"Thank you," she said with a smile. "We want at least five branches."

She elbowed him again when she heard him draw a breath.

The merchant gathered the branches, handing them to her after glancing at the earl.

She began to dig in her pocket for the money to pay him, shifting the branches so she could cradle them against her chest.

"I'll pay," the earl said in a gruff voice. He withdrew some change and handed it to the man, whose expression indicated that the amount was far more than expected.

"Let me get your change, sir," the merchant said.

"No need," the earl replied. "Happy holidays to you and your family," he added in a stilted tone.

The merchant's eyes widened, and he bowed as they walked away, Mr. Shorty straining at the leash.

"You didn't need to pay for them, you know," Pearl said in a low voice. "I am perfectly capable of paying my own way."

"And cracking your own eggs," he said in a voice that was far less gruff than before. Nearly amused, if she had to describe it.

"Precisely."

"How does your family celebrate Christmas?" she asked. "Actually, no," she said before he could reply.

Did she not wish to know after all? That thought bothered him far more than it should.

"First I need to hear about your family. You haven't said anything about them. Except that your godmother is Lady Robinson." She hesitated. "And tell me. Is Lady Robinson . . . pleasant?"

He nearly barked out laughter at how discreet she was trying to sound, even though the way she'd phrased her question told him everything he needed to know about how she felt about his godmother.

"She is very forthright in her opinions," he said in a neutral tone. He felt her shift, as though dissatisfied. "And no, she is not pleasant at all. That is why I like her so much."

She froze, and then twisted to the side to glare up at him. "Please do not tell me you like me then."

"I won't," he said, without thinking.

Oh God.

"I mean, I wouldn't presume to say anything about my feelings." Which was true in general, not just about how he felt about her. "You asked about my godmother, and I told you. I did not mean to imply that I did not—" Damn it. He was mucking this up. How had he managed to succeed in the world thus far being so poor at human interaction?

His sisters would point out he had not succeeded.

He heard her make a noise. Was she upset?

"So the only way I will know that you feel anything about me is if you say nothing at all." She sounded far too amused for the chagrin he had in his chest. And then she confirmed her amusement by giggling.

"It is not funny. I greatly apologize for my offense."

She nudged him in the side. "I'm not offended. I believe

I mentioned I have a twin, Olivia? She is constantly saying things that could be taken as offense, but she means well. She is better, now that she is married, but—"

"I have sisters too," he blurted. "Three of them. Gwyneth, Bryn, and Nesta."

"Where are you? I mean, are you the oldest or youngest or somewhere in between?"

"I'm in between Bryn and Nesta. Gwyneth is the oldest, she is married, but lives nearby." *And brings all of her unmarried young lady friends to visit.* "Bryn is engaged to be married and Nesta is determined never to marry because, and I am quoting her, 'men are foolish.'"

She laughed. "Your sister Nesta and my sister Ida would have a lot in common." She paused. "Or *did* have a lot in common. Ida is married now, so presumably she doesn't think her husband is foolish."

He hadn't thought of it until now, and it shouldn't matter, but—*And you? Are you engaged to be married?* "Tell me about your sisters."

She gave an exasperated sigh. "They are wonderful, but they are just so much sometimes. That is why I was so pleased to be left behind."

Right. He hadn't asked before, for fear of upsetting her, but he didn't have that fear any longer.

"I meant to ask," he said. "Why were you left behind?"

"I was found to be too insane to spend time with my family at Christmas."

He froze.

"I'm joking!" she said. "Honestly, you are far too gullible."

It's not that, he wanted to say. *It's just that I have so little experience actually having a conversation with someone who isn't related to me that I don't know what to do. Even worse is that it is a lovely young lady with a lively wit and a penchant for puns.*

I have no idea how to behave.

"No, it is that my mother came to town to do shopping, and she was too engrossed in sorting out all the packages to remember to make sure I was in the carriage." There was a hint of loss there. As though it hurt that she had been the least important package that day.

And of course it *would* hurt. He had never had to feel that way—if anything, his mother and sisters treated him as though he were the most important person in their world, even Gwyneth and Bryn, who had their own gentlemen in their lives.

That's why it was such a relief to be here, away from the noise of their demands and constant prying into his life alongside the constant exhortations to take a bride—as though any woman he married would possibly pass muster in their eyes.

"And there was a moment there where I could have run after the carriage and stopped it," she continued. "Only I thought it might be nice to be alone for the first time in my life." She squeezed his arm. "And it is, only it's not good to be alone when you have no idea how to make food for yourself, and you have to make your own fire and such. Until yesterday, I had no idea how to stoke a fire, for goodness' sake." She sounded outraged. "Much less cook for myself, as you know. I am very grateful for your help, my lord. Thank you."

Grateful. He realized, in a white-hot moment of clarity, that he did not want gratitude.

Not that he knew what he wanted, but he strongly suspected what it might be, even though what it appeared he wanted was entirely untoward. And inappropriate.

His sisters would not recognize him at this moment.

She would not be grateful if she knew where his thoughts were going.

"When someone says 'thank you' it is customary to respond with 'you're welcome.'"

"Damn it," he blurted. She froze, clutching his arm tighter. He stopped as well, screwing his eyes shut in horrified embarrassment.

"I'm sorry," he said in a whisper. "I can't seem to say anything—"

He felt her hand on his mouth. The warmth of her palm against his lips. "Hush," she replied in a soft voice. "It is fine. I know what you mean."

I know what you mean. Nobody had ever said that to him before. Because nobody had ever known what he meant, as much because he didn't allow himself to say anything—for obvious reasons—as that what he did end up saying was always misunderstood.

He reached up and removed her hand, opening his eyes slowly and turning to face her. "Do you?" he asked, his fingers going to her face to cup her jaw.

Her mouth curled into a smile, and she nodded. "I do." She rose up on tiptoes and pressed her mouth against his. "Do you know what I mean?" she murmured against his lips.

Chapter Five

On the fifth day of Christmas,
my true love gave to me
Five branches of green holly

Oh. Well, she hadn't precisely planned to kiss the exceedingly attractive Welsh earl while shopping a busy London street, but it seemed to have happened.

She drew back, her eyes wide, staring up at him in shock. Shock at her own actions as well as shock at how much she wished to continue the shocking action.

But they were on a busy London street, and what's more, she was holding five branches of holly, which had already poked her neck when she leaned up to kiss him.

"Uh . . ." she said, feeling her cheeks warm. Feeling her whole body warm, in fact—perhaps she should have kissed someone rather than trying to learn how to stoke a fire. It definitely had the same warming results.

He blinked, and then shook his head as though he wished to clear it. "That was—" he began, then shook his head again.

"I know. I am sorry." Could one die of mortification? She

didn't think so, but at this moment she rather wished it were true.

"Don't be sorry," he said quickly. "It was unexpected. You were just trying to make me feel better." And then a wry smile curved his mouth. "And I do, so thank you."

She couldn't help but smile back, at how his obvious awkwardness dissipated when he was just speaking his mind.

"You're welcome," she said pointedly.

"You make it sound so easy," he replied, but she heard only humor in his tone.

"It is easy. You just open your mouth and speak," she said. "Oh! I asked you about how your family celebrated Christmas. That's an excellent opportunity to practice."

Silence for a long moment. She was almost about to nudge him when he spoke.

"It's like any other family occasion," he began. "Everyone comes to the estate, and we have an enormous meal, and exchange gifts."

He didn't sound as though it was a particularly pleasant memory. Or that it had any emotional resonance for him at all.

"But before, when my father was alive, it was different." He paused again, only this time Pearl knew he was merely gathering his thoughts.

"My father gave each of us an ornament one year. A dragon, which you probably don't know is representative of Wales. I have no idea why," he said as an aside. "I must have been about seven years old, and I carried that ornament around for months past Christmas. We put it on the tree every year since then." He gave an embarrassed chuckle. "I brought it with me here, actually."

That was so sweet it made her heart hurt. And he still insisted he didn't care about Christmas?

But she wouldn't question him on any of that. She suspected he would only retreat into his grumpy earlness.

"Shall we go home and decorate?" Pearl said, raising the holly branches. "Although I think we might need some ribbon." She shifted to peer around him. "I think I see a woman selling some up there. Just the thing we need."

If she hadn't wanted to kiss him before—which she had, clearly, since she'd done it—his story would have made her.

She was even more glad she'd acted on her impulse.

"Why do we need so much ribbon?" Owen queried as she sorted through the basket.

"For decorating the holly, silly."

He looked confused. "But I thought the holly *was* the decoration. So we're going to decorate the decoration? Where does it stop?"

She laughed, then picked up a plaid ribbon and reached up to drape it on his head. "My sister Ida would likely be able to work out the mathematical equation on where, precisely, the decorating would stop, but for me the answer is when we think the house will be decorated enough."

He took the ribbon off and held it out to her, a serious expression on his face. "Then I think we need more ribbon. And are we decorating both houses? Or just mine?"

"Yours. I am guessing my mother will be returning to fetch me soon." She glanced up at the sky. Sure enough, the threat of inclement weather was becoming more pronounced, with a few early snowflakes starting to fall. "Though she will not travel in this weather."

"Is there anything I can do? I know you likely wish to spend Christmas with your family."

She opened her mouth to reply—*of course I do*—but then snapped it shut again. Because if she spent Christmas with her family, he would be alone for Christmas. And he might shrug it off as not important, but her heart ached at the thought of his being all alone in Lady Robinson's house with only Mr. Shorty for company.

"Nothing to do," she replied instead, waving her hand in dismissal. The snow was coming down thicker now, speckling his dark hair with white. "Let's go home and take care of our decorating equation."

She kissed me. Owen rolled the words around in his head as they walked back to his godmother's town house. Lady Pearl had kissed him. It had been a quick kiss, the kind of kiss that would be customary between relations, but he felt anything but familial toward her.

He wanted to kiss her again, and kiss her thoroughly this time. He wanted to bathe in the sparkle of her eyes, the warmth of her smile, her delightful sense of humor.

And he'd shared the story of his father's ornament. Not something he thought he'd ever reveal to anyone—his own family didn't know he still had it. It was one of the few things he had gotten from his father besides tangled accounts and family responsibility.

"I think we're going to be snowed in," she said, looking up at the sky. A snowflake fell on her nose, and she laughed as she brushed it off.

"You should stay with me then," he said, not thinking about what he'd just said. "I mean—" he said, then stopped when he realized whatever he'd say would be inappropriate. No wonder he only felt truly comfortable when he was talking to Mr. Shorty. "It makes sense to conserve fuel and food, and I don't think you should be alone, and since I am more familiar with starting fires than you are, it makes sense for us to team up."

She would be totally within proper behavior if she slapped his face for his suggestion. And then this dream, this idyllic respite from constantly feeling under scrutiny, would fall away, and he would be himself again, not a gentleman who could share puns with a lady and ensure her well-being with food and warmth.

Please don't slap me, he pleaded silently as he waited for her reply.

"I did promise myself an adventure," she began. "And it is much more fun being adventurous with someone else, I've found." She peered up at the sky. "It will take my mother at least two and three-quarters days to return to London from when she discovers I am missing. She'll have to wander about our country home for at least half a day looking into canisters and under beds in case I've accidentally stuffed myself into something." Her exasperated tone echoed one he had used on several occasions. "And then she'll have to write letters to all of my sisters telling them I've gone missing, although she won't necessarily tell them to look for me in London." Another sigh. "So by my calculations, we have possibly two and a half, or even three days before I'm found." She met his gaze and smiled. "It appears I will be accepting your kind invitation, Owen." She bit her lip. "I will accept as long as you accept my apology for what happened earlier." Her cheeks were flushed, and he knew it wasn't entirely due to the cold.

"There is no apology needed," he said. "It's Christmastime, isn't it? The time for making merry and decorating your house with greenery, for some reason, and kissing people you've just met."

He heard her utter a sigh of relief. "Well. Yes. It is. And I think, Owen, that we are going to have a wonderful Christmas."

Pearl found after a time that she enjoyed telling someone what to do. She'd never had the experience before; usually, one of her more . . . *strident* sisters would make a demand, and then someone would scurry to comply.

Pearl would just wait, balancing the need for something with the need to be unnoticed. If she were noticed, then chances were good her mother would try to marry her off to some unpleasant gentleman, or one of her sisters would drag her into a situation she did not want to be in.

But she wanted to be here with Owen. And be noticed

by him. What's more, she discovered she was absolutely engaged in wanting to decorate the house for Christmas so it was beautiful and he could have the Christmas she knew he should have. Even if *he* didn't know it.

And she would have the Christmas she wanted—one where she was the focus of attention, where she wasn't thinking about when she could sneak away to have a moment for herself.

"Are we finished *yet?*" He was wrapping holly around a glass above a fireplace, which was blazingly stoked. Apparently *he* already knew how to stoke a fire.

They were in the largest of the sitting rooms, which they'd decided would be where they slept.

Pearl couldn't worry that if anyone discovered how she would be spending the next few days, she would be completely and entirely ruined.

She would rather be warm, fed, and ruined than freeze and starve in her own house.

Which she would tell anyone who dared to question her actions.

Besides which, if she were entirely ruined she wouldn't have to hear her mother rail against her spinsterhood. A bonus to being ruined. She knew several of her sisters had thought the same thing before surrendering their spinsterhood to their respective husbands, with whom they'd fallen in love.

One thing she knew she would *not* do was marry him, regardless of any kind of pressure to do so. Even if it was from him, to preserve her good name.

What kind of marriage would it be if it were based on her need for warmth and food rather than love?

A terrible one, she could answer that herself.

Plus he did not want to marry her. It was only yesterday that he'd been so rude. Now he was tolerating her because he couldn't very well let her starve, not when she'd asked for his help, but that was a long way from swapping vows in front of a clergyman.

Although . . . she let her mind drift to what it would be like if she were married to him. She'd be in Wales, far from everyone she knew. Far from London. She'd likely have the freedom to do what she wanted, which would mean being as active as she wished without being deemed "not ladylike" or "too energetic." As though it was a bad thing to have energy.

And she'd be married to *him*, he of the devastating smile and the breadth of shoulders and height.

She could take Mr. Shorty walking anytime she liked.

She should not think about all of that, most especially what it would be like to share his bed. Those long limbs flung over her as they slept, his stubble scratching her face.

Stop thinking.

"Pearl?" he sounded as abrupt as he had yesterday, abrupt and annoyed, and she realized she'd kept him waiting. He stood in front of the fireplace, gesturing to the holly. "Finished? Are we?"

"Oh yes, of course." She nodded enthusiastically. "It looks lovely. You did a lovely job."

He looked heavenward as if asking for patience.

"Lovely," he repeated, and she folded her arms over her chest and glared at him and his dismissive tone.

"Look, Owen, this is so you have a semblance of a Christmas, even though you said you don't care."

He flung his hands up. "I *don't* care. I don't know why you do."

She stomped toward him, not sure what she was going to do when she reached him.

His eyes widened as she approached. So he didn't know what she was going to do either.

They had that in common.

"I care," Pearl said, poking a finger in his chest, "because it is obvious you are a curmudgeon, and you need to find some joy in your life."

He raised an eyebrow as he wrapped his hand around the offending finger. "Curmudgeon?" He sounded amused now.

"Mmm-hmm." This close, she was keenly aware of how much bigger he was than she. Taller, wider, stronger.

"I need to find some joy?" he said. His eyes drifted to her mouth, and it felt as though he were kissing her.

Her breath caught.

"You do."

He stared at her for a moment longer, then shook his head and blinked a few times. She tried not to feel disappointed that he hadn't kissed her.

And then decided she didn't want to be disappointed, especially at this time of year.

Owen froze as she put her hands on his shoulders, using him to raise herself up on her tiptoes.

Was she—?

And then her lips curled into a half-smile, and she brushed his mouth with hers. "Joy," she whispered, before kissing him again.

He wrapped his arms around her while leaning back against the fireplace mantle, shifting so he was lower and she was higher. That made it so she was effectively leaning on him so she could better reach his mouth.

Which, it seemed, she wanted to do.

Even though, it also seemed, she wasn't quite sure what to do now that their mouths were pressed together.

He drew back, just enough to be able to speak. "Do you want me to—?" he began.

"Yes," she said in a breathy voice. "Yes, I want you to kiss me. I want you to teach me how to kiss."

"And this will bring you joy?" he said, unable to resist teasing her. Even though he never teased anyone—his sisters would say he didn't have a humorous bone in his body, but not only was that not true, he absolutely did not want to be thinking about his sisters right now.

"It will. Hurry up, damn it," she said, and he suppressed a laugh before lowering his mouth to hers.

He wasn't an expert in kissing by any means, but he had some experience in the activity. And he knew kissing her would bring him joy—if "joy" was currently the feeling of passion that was spreading through his entire body, not to mention his trousers—and he wanted to bring her joy as well.

He opened his mouth to lick at the seam of her lips. He heard her gasp, and his tongue slid in, gently, in case this was not what she wanted.

But it seemed it was.

Because in the next second, her tongue had met his, and she was enthusiastically participating in the event.

He tightened his grip on her, and she did the same, sliding her hands across his shoulders to his neck. Sliding her fingers into his hair as she kept kissing him.

She was a fast learner. And, not coincidentally, he was fast becoming aroused.

It would not do to continue this, especially given that they were currently alone in the house and had plans to share a room.

Stop, he told himself. Yet unable to for a moment as she kissed him more thoroughly, making a soft noise in her throat.

But he must, or this would go in an irrevocable direction. One neither one of them wanted. Which he would tell himself until his . . . *want* subsided.

He set her back on her feet, already missing the feel of her body against his. "I think that's enough joy for now," he said, his words ragged.

She met his gaze, keeping her eyes locked on his for a long moment until she nodded her head in agreement. "Yes," she replied, and she sounded breathless too, "probably enough joy for the evening."

She swallowed, then nodded again and stepped back. "Uh—so I will just go get the ribbons." She swallowed again, and then she spun on her heel and walked out of the room, her back rigid.

Only the ribbons were lying on the table in front of the sofa, not outside of the room.

He suppressed a grin as he waited for her return.

Chapter Six

On the sixth day of Christmas
my true love gave to me
Six ribbons, one of which was green

Pearl winced as she realized the ribbons were not actually in the room she'd just gone into. They were back there with *him*.

With the large grumpy gentleman she'd just kissed—and who had just kissed her—and who didn't seem to be all that grumpy anymore.

More joyful, in fact, if she had to describe his demeanor.

Kissed. She'd been kissed. By him, a stranger until yesterday. A man who was only visiting London, who had made no mention of any kind of attachment back home in Wales, who could be married, for all she knew.

God, please don't let him be married.

She spun on her heel and marched back in, an icy feeling gripping her spine.

He was waiting for her, an amused look on his face. Was he laughing at how inexperienced a kisser she was? Or was he laughing at himself because he had kissed her, even though he found her completely unattractive?

"The ribbons are here," he said, gesturing to where they were neatly draped over his arm.

"Are you married?" she blurted out, then clapped her hand over her mouth. She hadn't intended to just say it, but then again, she'd had so little experience with being given the space to speak—what with having four very lively sisters, all of whom wanted to share their thoughts—that she was inexperienced at that too.

His eyes widened and his smile faltered. "No, of course not. Would I have kissed you if I were—oh, never mind," he said, shaking his head.

"Many gentlemen do," she replied in a quieter voice. At least he wasn't married. "And I kissed *you*, remember."

"I'm not many gentlemen," he retorted, then uttered a derisive snort. "Something I think you might have noticed by now." He sounded rueful. "And I was an active participant in the kiss." He paused, then spoke in a low tone. "Are you? I know you're not married, but are you engaged?"

Pearl shook her head before he finished the question. "No, thank goodness." But she did not want to get into that sticky subject with him, the most attractive man she'd ever seen, let alone kissed.

Since she'd never kissed anyone before.

She took a deep breath and walked toward him. "Hand me that green ribbon. I want to do this right."

He drew the ribbon from his arm and held it to her. She took it and walked past him to the holly branches. Then wrinkled her nose as she regarded what they'd done. "There's not nearly enough holly." She turned back to look at him. "We should get some more and see if anyone has a tree for sale."

He looked at her as though she were insane. Perhaps she was.

But she'd just had her first kiss. A woman was allowed to be a teensy bit insane after that had occurred.

"A tree? I have no need of a tree."

She regarded him for a moment, tilting her head. "I believe you do. You have an ornament already, don't you? What's more, I imagine your doctor would want you to as well. Because," she began, turning back around so she could thread the ribbon through the holly, willing herself to speak in a conversational tone, not one that would indicate how breathless she was currently feeling, "having a tree, celebrating Christmas, can only put you in a more amenable mood. And I know that being in a pleasant mood will help your recovery." She tied the ribbon in a bow, then stepped back to look at the work. "Not ideal, it needs a lot more, but it is a start. Don't you think?" she asked, looking over her shoulder at him.

He was staring at her as though he couldn't believe his ears. So he was consistent in finding her impossible.

That should bode well for their future dealings.

"We are not getting a tree."

She raised her eyebrow. Now that she knew he wasn't married and that he seemed to feel vulnerable, he felt much more approachable.

Besides which, they had kissed already, so that should mean *something* in terms of familiarity.

Not to mention they'd be sharing a room this evening.

Oh dear.

"We should go before the snowstorm gets truly bad. Mr. Shorty has to go out anyway, doesn't he?"

She didn't wait for his answer, but went to where she'd folded her cloak up and began to put it on. "Hurry up."

He moved as though he were in shock, putting his coat on and then leaning down to snap Mr. Shorty's leash on.

At least he wasn't still giving her that "you are an insane woman" look.

A tree, of all things. Because Christmas, of course. And here Owen thought he had left managing ladies behind when he'd left Wales.

But there was something endearing about how she wanted to lift his spirits. Even though he knew himself to be a grump.

Or, more accurately, his spirits might be lifted for a few moments—for example, when he was kissing a delightfully appealing woman—but he would return to his usual demeanor in a while. His sister Bryn called it "throwing an Owen," which wasn't nearly as clever as she thought it was. Because it didn't really rhyme.

Perhaps he should present the phrase to Pearl, to see if she could come up with something better. She seemed to appreciate a good pun after all. Something they had in common.

Had he ever thought that about a female who wasn't related to him?

Actually, he didn't think it all that often about the females who were related to him. They saw him as the head of the family, the perpetual provider, the man they tried to lead around as though he was a sheep and they were the sheepdogs.

Only he would not be led. Not into being polite, not into fancy clothing, and definitely not into marriage.

"Owen?" She sounded impatient. Of course, because he'd been woolgathering—ha!—for the last five minutes.

"Right. We're getting a tree because you insist it will improve my spirits." He didn't try to keep the dismissiveness from his tone.

"Have you read Mr. Dickens's story *A Christmas Carol?*" she asked, in such a deliberately innocent tone he knew there was something she wasn't saying.

"No. Why?"

She shrugged. "Nothing. Just you seem like a particular character in the story, I was wondering if Mr. Scrooge was actually a sheepish Welsh earl."

He smothered a snort of laughter at "sheepish." He didn't want to let her know, not now at least, that she amused him.

Even though she absolutely did.

The snow was coming down so quickly the sidewalks and roads almost had a chance to be white before getting walked or driven over, turning the accumulation to a dingy mush.

The snow had gathered on her hair, which he'd just realized wasn't covered by a hat. Didn't ladies usually wear hats?

But this lady was unlike any he'd met before, so perhaps this lady did not wear a hat.

"We have to hope we find a seller soon," she said, brushing snowflakes off her nose with her left hand. Her right was once again tucked in his arm, helping to steady him as they walked through the slippery snow. He barely needed his cane.

"Oh no," he replied in mock dismay. "What will we ever do if we can't find a tree?"

She turned to glare at him. "We are going to have fun, Owen, even if it kills you."

"It just might," he murmured, but he didn't mean it. Today and yesterday felt like a long dream, one where he was understood and someone wanted him to celebrate the holiday just because it was fun, not because they would get something out of it.

"There!" she exclaimed, increasing her pace so she pulled him along after her.

A man stood next to a cart that was half-filled with trees, glancing worriedly up at the sky. Of course, the merchant only had one day left to sell his trees before Christmas, and this bad weather was bound to discourage some shoppers.

Not them, though.

"Hello, sir," she called as they walked up to the cart. "We would like to purchase a tree."

"You've come to the right place," the man said, a wide grin on his face. He gestured toward his cart. "I can show you any type you like, tall or short, skinny or fat."

"Just show us the tree that looks most Christmassy," she replied.

Owen shook his head at that lack of description, but it appeared the man knew what she was talking about, since he dragged one tree off the cart and stood it up, stamping its trunk on the ground while turning it. "That one there."

Owen looked at the tree, unable to tell what made it more or less Christmassy than the others. Now that it seemed he was committed to this course of action, he would let her take the lead. That was unusual for him—normally he was the one who had to make all the decisions. It was a relief to be able to follow someone else for a change.

"Yes, that is perfect," she said in approval.

Owen withdrew his wallet from his coat and handed over some bills. "Thank you."

The man glanced at the bills, then looked back up at him. "Do you need it delivered? I'm just finishing up here anyway, need to get home before the storm makes it impossible."

Owen shook his head. "No, thank you. We'll carry it home ourselves."

"Are you certain I can't help?" Pearl asked for what seemed like the hundredth time. She brushed snow off his shoulders, as though that would ease his burden.

Plus she liked touching his shoulders.

"It's fine," he said in his grumpy earl voice.

"But it's so heavy!" she replied. She gestured with his cane, which he'd passed to her when he'd taken the tree.

"It's fine."

"You're stubborn, do you know that?" she asked. "And your leg and shoulder are hurt. I am certain your doctor would disapprove."

He stopped walking, turning to look at her. He didn't look as grumpy as he sounded. If anything, he looked—nearly delighted?

"Look, I know you want to make this a wonderful Christmas for me. And I appreciate that. But one of the things that I am accustomed to doing is . . . doing for others." He gestured to the tree with the hand that wasn't holding the trunk. "And this is doing for you and making me have a wonderful Christmas. It serves two purposes. Like sheep. Milk and wool," he explained, presumably in answer to her puzzled expression. "And when we get home, I promise I will rest my leg. But let me do this now."

"Oh." It explained a lot, actually, his talking about doing for others. He knew how to build a fire, knew how to make eggs, knew how to drag trees across town—not that he'd likely ever done that before.

"Do you do for others often? In which case, I should be the one hauling the tree so you could have a well-deserved rest."

"It's a little late to be asking that question now that we're nearly home," he said in a dry tone of voice.

She glanced up. She hadn't realized how close they were—they just had to turn around the next corner and they'd be on their street heading to their—no, his—no, Lady Robinson's town house.

"You didn't answer the question."

Owen paused in the middle of affixing a candle to one of the branches of the tree. *Their* tree. He was kneeling on the floor with branches poking him in the face, but he was determined to finish the task she'd set out for him. "Didn't answer what?"

She tilted her head, a candle in each hand. They'd scoured the house for as many as they could find. Pearl was apparently determined to set the house on fire. Or, as she put it, decorate the tree the same way Queen Victoria and Prince Albert did.

"Do you do for others often?"

The question made Owen pause. Nobody had ever asked him that before.

"Yes." He put the candle on the floor and leaned back, stretching his injured leg out in front of him. He let out an involuntary groan as he did, which made her hurry to his side, kneeling down as she placed her candles next to his.

"See, I knew you shouldn't have dragged that tree." She went to place her hands on his leg, then hesitated. "May I?" she asked in a soft voice. "I found when my own leg was injured that it was helpful to have someone rub the injury."

They'd already engaged in such scandalous behavior it wouldn't matter one way or the other if she touched him. "Go ahead," he said, wincing at the pain. He really had overdone it, and if he were less bound by his own honor and his pride at being able to do something for her, he would not have dragged that damned tree home.

But her eyes had lit up when she'd seen it, and he didn't want to have anyone see their unusual—albeit temporary—living quarters.

"Ahh," he said when her fingers gripped his leg. Her hands wrapped around his calf completely, and she began to knead it, gazing at him with a concerned expression.

"Is this too much?" she asked.

"No, it feels wonderful." He leaned his head back and closed his eyes, focusing on what she was doing. There was nothing remotely sexual about her touch, but the fact that she had seen him in pain and rushed to do something about it was incredibly appealing.

"I might have mentioned, I had a cricket injury a few summers back," she said, her fingers still working his leg muscle. "And my twin, Olivia, was determined to relieve my pain, so she sent our other sister Ida to research what might help."

"Ida is your intelligent sister? Your version of my sister Bryn?"

"If Bryn likes to display her knowledge at any moment on the slightest provocation, then yes," Pearl replied dryly.

He laughed, then winced as she hit a particularly sore spot.

"Too much?" she asked. It seemed she was keeping a close eye on his reactions. He wasn't used to that either. It felt good, nearly as good as her touch did.

"No, it's good. Just a bit more, I don't want it to get sore."

"Of course." She worked in silence for a few more moments, then removed her hands. He opened his eyes to see her leaning back on the floor.

"Thank you," he said. "That has definitely eased the pain."

He made as if to stand up, only to have her hold her hand out in a "stop" gesture.

"No, you go lie on the couch. I'll finish the candles."

"But—" he began, and she shook her head. Definitively. As she seemed to do often. He did like that about her, that she was so decided.

In fact, he would have to admit, he liked *her.*

"No. I want you to have a nice Christmas, not one filled with pain."

"So don't invite my mother," he murmured as he made his way upright.

"And definitely don't invite mine," she said, her tone rueful. She took his arm and guided him to the couch, then settled him as comfortably as he was able. Thank goodness the couch was long enough to accommodate his height. "Oh! And you mentioned that ornament, a dragon? I can go get it and hang it on the tree, if you like."

It touched him that she'd remembered. "It's upstairs in the second room on the right. That's been my bedroom. It should be on the dresser. I can go up and get it," he added, beginning to sit up.

"No, let me. I can fetch an ornament, for goodness' sake." She sounded irritated, and he smothered a grin.

She went upstairs and returned a few minutes later, holding the dragon. "This is it?"

She held it out to him, and he took it, their fingers brushing. It was made of wood, and clearly old and worn; one of the jeweled eyes had fallen out, and the tail was bent, but it still evoked memories, good memories, of his father and Christmases past.

"Do you want to hang it?" she asked.

He handed it back to her. "No, you. Just there where I can see it lying on the couch."

He watched as she approached the tree, glancing back at him to confirm the dragon was in the position he most wanted. He nodded, and she returned to him, clearly about to get him into his position as well.

"No, not that," he exclaimed as she drew a knitted throw from where it lay on one of the other chairs. "I'm not an invalid."

She laughed, tossing the throw back where it had been. "I see, so your firm limit is that you absolutely will not allow yourself to be covered with a blanket. You might want to reconsider that, Owen, when it's time for bed."

And then they both froze. "Bed." The word hung there, between them, and their gazes met. He wanted to reassure her that she would be safe with him, but then again, he couldn't speak.

"It will be fine," she said after a moment. "I know you're concerned for my reputation, but nobody will ever know. Nobody notices me." She shrugged, as though it didn't matter. *Of course it matters,* he wanted to say. "My mother is focused on marrying me off, but as long as I am back in our own house when she arrives, she won't notice a thing. She is not the most observant person." Owen felt his chest constrict—in sympathy?—at her tone. Not her joyful, determined, "I will devour cheese and bread in your kitchen" tone. Lost, as though she was just waiting to be noticed.

He noticed her. But he didn't want to give her the wrong impression by telling her that, particularly after reminding one another that they would be spending the night in the same house. The same *room*, given that it didn't make sense to have two fires going, not when they weren't sure how long the snowstorm would last.

"Anyway," she continued, speaking in a brusque tone, "I'll finish the candles and then I'll go make supper."

"You?" he said, sounding skeptical. Not unreasonable, given she had just been taught how to crack an egg.

"Yes, me," she replied. She sounded determined. Again. "It shouldn't be too difficult. Just let me do for you for a moment, Owen."

Chapter Seven

On the seventh day of Christmas
my true love gave to me
Seven delicious kisses

Pearl glared at the eggs in the bowl, which were studded with bits of eggshell.

"Need some assistance?"

She twisted around to see Owen, who was standing in the doorway, one shoulder propped against the jamb.

"I am fine," she replied, raising her chin.

He walked into the room, leaning on his cane. His limp was more pronounced, and she felt guilty all over again—she shouldn't have insisted they have a tree, much less allow him to drag it home.

"I think you need help. It's perfectly acceptable to ask for help, Pearl."

"Oh, like you do?" she snapped back. Then her eyes widened as she realized how sharp she'd been.

He froze. "You're right. I don't ask for help. How about we both learn how to do it? I'll go first. 'Pearl, can you help me walk my dog? He needs to go out, and I fear it is too snowy for me to manage.'"

She leaned to one side to peer out one of the high windows that looked out onto the back garden. Sure enough, the snow was coming down even more thickly, piling up into soft white drifts.

"And now you," he prodded.

She exhaled exaggeratedly, then crossed her arms over her chest. "Fine. Owen, will you help me make dinner?"

He held his arms out wide. "See? That wasn't so hard."

Mr. Shorty trotted into the kitchen as though on cue.

"We can just let him out into the back garden, but I wasn't certain I could go fetch him if he didn't return after he finished," Owen explained.

"Ah, I see."

He walked past her to the other end of the kitchen and unlatched a small door—too small for him without ducking his head—and opened it just a bit, but still enough to let swirls of snow pour in.

Mr. Shorty scooted quickly outside, and Owen shut the door behind him.

"He'll be all right out there?" Pearl asked.

"He will," Owen assured her. "I'll open the door in about ten minutes; he shouldn't need any longer than that." He walked back toward her. "Now show me what you're making."

They salvaged dinner, although they were low on eggs, so they had to make do with the ones Pearl had already cracked. Mr. Shorty was eager to return back inside—likely because his little legs were sinking into the snowdrifts—so Pearl didn't have to go out and rescue him. He tracked snow all over the kitchen, making the floor slippery, so Pearl insisted that Owen take a seat and direct her activities so he wouldn't slip and fall.

It was so cozy and domestic, not as though either one of them usually had servants to take care of everything. As though they belonged together doing cozy, domestic things.

It felt scarily right.

"It's just that I didn't realize the shells were so fragile!" Pearl explained for what seemed the hundredth time after Owen made a face while eating.

"No, it's not that," he said.

They were back in their room, sitting side by side on the large sofa Owen had been lying on earlier. The scorned throw was on Pearl's lap, while Mr. Shorty was on Owen's.

"What then?"

"I think I had you heat the pan up too long so the butter got burnt. That's my fault, not yours," he said. He waved his hand. "But it's fine, as long as you haven't noticed."

She hadn't. Mostly because she was enjoying herself too much to notice anything about their dinner—Owen had finished the eggs, while Pearl had collected all the cheeses she could find, placing them on a platter that was stored high above her head, requiring Owen's help to retrieve. A quick wash later—and Pearl was embarrassed at how proud she was of actually washing a dish—and she was arranging the cheese in color order, from the palest cheddar to . . . the darkest cheddar.

"Your godmother is very fond of cheddar," she observed. "Not that I blame her, it is delicious."

Owen leaned forward to take one of the bits from the platter, popping it into his mouth. "Mm," he murmured.

She felt her breath catch at the sight of his pleasure. Oh lord. He was gorgeous when grumpy, of course. Still gorgeous when being pleasant, as he had been this entire day, save for the maligned throw incident. But when he was enjoying himself? When his eyes fluttered closed as his strong jaw chewed, his mouth moving, the cords in his neck shifting?

Was there a word stronger than "gorgeous"? "Gorgeousest"? Ida would know, but thankfully Ida wasn't here. Only Pearl was. Here to savor every moment with this handsome man, to have conversations she doubted either one of them had ever had.

"Do I have something on my face?" he asked, startling her out of her reverie.

"Uh—" she began, feeling her cheeks start to heat.

His brows drew together as though in concern. "You're not feeling ill, are you?" He shook his head before she could reply. "I knew we shouldn't have gone out in this weather."

"No, you ridiculous man," Pearl said at last. He kept staring at her with that concerned expression. It touched her that he was worried about her.

Had anybody who wasn't one of her sisters ever been worried about her?

She knew the answer to that question.

"It's none of that. It's that—it's that I want more joy," she said in a low voice before leaning over to him and placing her mouth on his.

She was kissing him. Again.

It was awkward because they were seated next to each other on the sofa, and Mr. Shorty was on his lap, shifting in reaction as she leaned into him. Owen scooped his dog up without breaking the kiss—an impressive feat, he had to admit—and lowered him gently to the floor, then wrapped his other arm around Pearl, drawing her nearer.

She wriggled closer, and then put her hand on his face to hold his jaw, angling him into a better position for a kiss.

He liked how . . . determined she was.

She drew away, and he suppressed whatever disappointment he felt.

"Is this—is this acceptable?" she said in a whisper. "Because I just—I mean, it's that you—?" and then she shook her head, sending hair spilling around her face.

"This is more than acceptable, Pearl." He spoke in a hushed tone of voice. "I want to kiss you more than anything."

She smiled, that lovely wholehearted smile, her eyes crinkling at the corners. "Good. I just wanted to make certain."

"That you weren't taking undue advantage of me?" he said, humor threading through his voice. "Thank you."

"Thank *you*," she murmured, before returning her lips to his.

This kiss was slower, less frantic than before. Perhaps

because she had explicitly asked if he wanted it? And had likewise communicated her enthusiasm?

And there was also the truth that they were here, together, for the foreseeable future.

So they could take their time.

Owen placed his fingers at her waist, feeling the warmth of her on his skin. She had slid her hand from his jaw to the side of his head, cradling it in her palm. He made a moan deep in his throat when she raked her nails on his scalp, then slid her hand down his neck, over his collarbone, to rest at his chest. He placed his other hand on top of hers, moving it so her palm skimmed across his nipple underneath his shirt. He wished he could just remove his shirt entirely, but he did not want to stop kissing her, nor did he want to scare her with how quickly things were proceeding.

Also, he was likely to be cold, given that it was storming outside and he hadn't stoked the fire since before dinner.

Her fingers were hesitant, but then more insistent, finding his nipple and rubbing it, and he made that groan in his throat again. As much to encourage her as to express his appreciation.

She was the aggressor in their kiss now, sliding her tongue into his mouth and tangling it with his. He felt her shift on the couch, and then she had somehow raised herself up and eased herself onto his lap, facing him directly.

Her body rested on his thighs, and once again he resisted the urge to draw her closer, to place her bottom directly on top of his hardening cock.

And then she shot backward and would have tumbled off his lap if he hadn't caught her.

"Oh my god," she said, her eyes wide, "am I hurting your leg?" She scrambled off him back onto the couch, the skirt of her gown hiking up just enough for him to see her calves. "You shouldn't have let me do that, I could hurt you."

Owen stretched his arm out on the back of the sofa and put his fingers on her shoulder, stroking the soft skin there. He shook his head. "My leg is only injured below the knee. I promise, I will speak up for myself if I feel that I am in danger."

"Oh."

Her face was flushed, whether from the kissing or the embarrassment of the kissing, of course he didn't know.

"It was lovely, Pearl," he said in a low voice. "You made me forget the pain, made me forget everything while you were kissing me."

Her cheeks were blazing red now, so he could safely assume her heated reaction was to the embarrassment, not the kissing.

She licked her lips, and he froze. The sight of her tongue darting out to spread moisture on her mouth—well, he'd have to be the most unimaginative man in the world not to think about what else she could lick.

Stop that, Owen, he reminded himself. *This young lady is temporarily in your care. It is your responsibility to ensure she is kept safe.*

"I can sleep in another room," he said, but her head was shaking no before he could even finish.

"No, if anything, I should sleep in another room. Clearly—" and she spread her hands out to indicate them and the couch "—I am not to be trusted around you."

He repressed a chuckle at how earnest she sounded.

"We are both reasonable people. There is no one else here. At least," he continued, glancing down at Mr. Shorty, "nobody who will say anything. We can do whatever we like. Or not do. And I will tell you if you do anything that I do not like."

She kept her gaze on him, her expression reserved. He could tell she was thinking it all out, and wondered at her saying that one of her other sisters was the intelligent one—clearly, Pearl was very smart. And thoughtful, considerate, kind, and determined.

Damn it. He already thought better of her than any other female he was not related to, and he'd only known her two days.

What would happen if they were snowed in until Christmas?

Chapter Eight

On the eighth day of Christmas
my true love gave to me
Eight ways to distract me
(from kissing him)

Pearl was seriously considering running outside to plant her face in the snow so it would cool down. She felt as though she was a stoked fire herself, which perhaps, given what she'd just done—*what she'd just done!*—she might be.

"Pearl?" His voice came as though through a fog, distantly reaching her through her tumbling thoughts.

"Yes."

"Are you all right?"

Other than worrying she might explode in a passionate conflagration?

"Yes, I am fine. I was just thinking."

"Don't think too hard," he said, humor lacing his tone.

She snorted. She couldn't help herself. "I've seen how you look, you can't tell me you don't think all the time."

He made a dismissive gesture. "Yes, of course, but I can offer you advice I don't take."

She appreciated how he was deliberately trying to relieve the situation with humor. Even if his humor was acknowledging that he refused to do what would be best for him—doing for others instead.

She glanced at the clock in the corner. Which was no help, since it had obviously stopped some time before. No servants were there to wind it after all.

"It's probably close to nine," he said, noticing where she was looking. "Are you getting tired?"

Not really, but then again, right now I feel as though I could stay up for the rest of my life, as long as I have you to talk to.

"Yes," she said, imbuing her words with a determination she did not feel.

"I can take this couch, and you can have the other one over there."

She got up and walked to the couch he'd indicated, beginning to drag it closer to the fire.

"Wait, let me help," he said.

She stopped her movement and gave him a forbidding look. "You are not to further injure yourself. I am strong, I can do this myself."

"But—"

"No."

She didn't wait for him to continue arguing, she just made short work of what she'd been doing, bringing it within a few feet of the fire, which was also within a few feet of his couch. They both had a good view of the tree.

"The eye of the dragon catches the light," she remarked as she sat down on her sofa.

"Mm."

"I like that you told me about the ornament. Do you take it with you always?"

An exhale. "I do. It—it feels like home. As though as long as it is here with me, I am home. Even if home is an empty town house in London."

"Not so empty now."

"For which I'm quite pleased."

She smiled at his firm tone.

"We'll need blankets," she said, getting up again. "I'll go find them."

"You won't accept my help," he said. It was not a question.

"No, I will not. You and Mr. Shorty stay there."

She returned about half an hour later, blankets and linens piled up high in her arms. It felt rather empowering to do things like this for oneself, even though that was a ridiculously privileged thing to think—after all, there were very few women who didn't do things like this as part of their daily routine. It was just that Pearl was one of the privileged few, which meant that everyday things like finding one's cloak, cracking an egg, and locating blankets were out of her range of experience.

Kissing a man.

Not that she thought women who weren't duke's daughters did that all the time—just that she was usually so protected, so chaperoned, that there wasn't even that possibility.

Nor were any of the men she'd met in fashionable ballrooms gentlemen she would like to kiss anyway.

He was still on the couch, Mr. Shorty now on his chest. One of his large hands was petting his dog, while his other was flung behind his head.

"You look nearly comfortable," she remarked as she walked toward him. She bent down to place the stack in her arms on the floor. "Do you want linens and a blanket? Drat, I didn't think to get pillows, I can just go—"

"I don't need a pillow," he said, interrupting. "You've done far too much already."

"I've barely done anything," she retorted. "You're the one who got the fire going, told me how to make our dinner, and had food in the first place."

He waved his hand. "That's what I do."

"So you've said." She took the top blanket off the stack and shook it out, then lay it over him and Mr. Shorty, who quickly escaped onto the floor, coming up to her with a pleading expression on his face.

"He wants cheese. Do not give it to him or we will be regretting it all night."

"Why—oh!" she said, putting her hand over her mouth to suppress her laughter.

"Precisely."

Owen drew the blanket further up his body, tucking it right under his chin. He looked funny lying there, completely covered except for his face.

His gorgeous, rakishly unshaven face.

"I don't need anything else," he said after a moment. She realized she must have been standing there staring at him. Oops.

"Right, yes, well, I will take the linens here and then this blanket," she said in a hurried tone, walking over to her couch to begin making her bed.

"Will you need help with—with?" he asked in an awkward tone.

"With—oh!" she said. "Uh . . ." she began.

"I've done it before for my sisters."

"Is there anything you can't do?" she said, wishing she didn't sound so peevish.

He chuckled. "Well, apparently I can't offer to help a lady undo her gown without raising her hackles." He shook his head. "That sounded far more inappropriate when I said it aloud."

"You weren't inappropriate, I promise. You were just responding to me. I didn't mean to be rude."

He exhaled, as though in relief. "Well, thank goodness. It's fine. No offense taken on either side."

How much time had he spent reassuring her thus far? *It's fine you gobbled up my cheese, that you made me take your arm, that you kissed me.*

"Come over here," he said in a low voice after a few moments.

She walked toward him, a hesitant expression on her face. He wanted to reassure her that he had nothing on his mind beyond helping her undo her gown, even though that would be a lie.

But it would be truth to say he wouldn't do anything except help her undo her gown so she could sleep more comfortably.

This had to be the oddest situation he'd ever been in.

It was also one of the most intriguing.

And he didn't know how long it would last—when her family would come to collect her, when he'd be sufficiently healed to return home—but he would savor every moment.

"Turn around," he said, when she had stopped in front of him. He rose up from the sofa, his fingers going to the back of her gown. There were several tiny buttons studding the back.

"How did you do this last night?"

"I didn't," she said. "It was not comfortable, which is why I don't wish to repeat it." She made a noise indicating frustration. "These few days are showing me, in painful clarity, why I wouldn't be nearly as brave as my sister Della." She twisted her head to look at him. "She's the one who ran away. We thought she'd eloped, but she hadn't."

"Your sisters are far more adventurous than mine," he observed. His fingers were about midway down her back undoing the buttons. The two halves of the gown began to fall to their respective sides, revealing her corset and chemise. "You're done," he said hastily, not wanting to tempt himself even more. "How is your sister braver than you?" he asked, as much to distract himself from the sight of her skin as to hear her answer. "Does she undo her own buttons by some miraculously flexible trick?"

She laughed as she returned to her sofa, sitting down and bringing her blanket up over her. He could see her body squirming underneath, and knew she was taking her gown off.

"Della knows how to do things. Not just undoing her own gown, but paying her bills, making friends, and taking charge of her life." She paused. "Though it took her some time to figure it all out."

He saw her draw her gown up over the blanket, then she laid it on the opposite sofa arm.

He lay back down, bringing his own blanket up. "What would you do if you knew all these things? What kind of life would you have?"

He heard her shifting on the sofa, then glanced over to see she too was lying down, her blanket tucked in around her.

Mr. Shorty was in the middle, glancing between them as though trying to figure out which person to go lie on.

Eventually he trotted over to Pearl's sofa and jumped up, somewhat awkwardly, settling himself on her chest.

"Traitor," Owen said, but in an amused tone.

"I've been so focused on what I don't want to do that I haven't thought about what I would do," Pearl replied in a thoughtful voice. She pulled her arm out from underneath the blankets and began to pet Mr. Shorty.

"We have time. Unless you're sleepy?" he asked quickly. He didn't want her to stay up and talk to him just because he wasn't tired.

"I'm not." She spoke with the definitiveness he was coming to admire more and more. "I need to think about that for a minute."

He heard her shifting again, then he heard Mr. Shorty make a noise of protest. "When I first realized I was alone, truly alone, I could only think about small things. Like skating in the hallways or jumping on the beds. I went out to a café and bought a hot chocolate. All by myself." A pause. "Pathetic, really."

"Not pathetic at all," Owen shot back. "The things that immediately came to your mind can reveal a lot about yourself, if you analyze it."

"Hm," she said, sounding skeptical.

"Let me explain. You mentioned playing cricket earlier, and two of the three things you wanted to do involved physical activity. So obviously you feel constricted in your current life, and you wish you had the freedom to run around and be yourself. Am I right?"

"You are." She sounded shocked, and he resisted the urge to preen. Mostly because supine preening wasn't a skill he'd yet mastered.

"And the hot chocolate?" she asked.

"Obviously you enjoy the simple pleasures of life—hot chocolate, the many varieties of Cheddar cheese, the warmth of a very good dog. Am I right?" he asked again.

He heard her chuckle. "You are. Only I was so disappointed in the hot chocolate, it had lumps." She sounded sleepily outraged, which made him smile.

"We should do something to rectify that. You should at

least have a reasonable hot chocolate before you return to your usual life."

"That sounds wonderful," she murmured, and he could tell she was falling asleep.

He waited, listening to the crackling of the fire, to his own heartbeat, to Mr. Shorty's occasional gurgles and snorts, before drifting off to sleep himself.

Chapter Nine

On the ninth day of Christmas
my true love gave to me
Nine offers of perfectly made tea

Pearl tossed the blanket off, hearing a yelp as it apparently landed on Mr. Shorty. She glanced across to the other sofa, where she could see his limbs stirring. "Good morning!" she called.

"Umph," he groaned, rolling over so his back was to her.

"It's Christmas Eve! Owen, we have to go out and do things." What things, she wasn't certain. Just that it was very likely today would be the last day of this crazy dreamtime, and she wanted to make the most of it.

"What things?" he growled. Had he read her mind?

She flung her arms up. "Things! Christmas things! And you promised me hot chocolate, didn't you?"

He rolled back around to glare at her. His stubble was even darker, and his hair was all messed up, making him look even more dangerously rakish than before. And also unkempt.

She liked unkempt.

"You are unnaturally sprightly in the morning," he said in a disgusted voice.

She grinned at how drolly grumpy he sounded.

"You sound just like my twin. Olivia," she clarified.

"Is your twin this annoying in the morning?" He was trying to sound grumpy, but she could hear his amusement.

She grinned even more. Had she—Pearl Howlett, of the infamous duke's daughters—ever gotten anyone so irked before? Besides her twin, of course.

She had not. She was the *not* sister, after all, so her impression on anybody was likely to be a negative—as in, she hadn't run off and caused scandal, she wasn't loudly declaiming her intelligence, nor was she arguing with everyone in sight.

But here she was actually affecting someone. Annoying them, to be sure, but affecting them nonetheless.

"Can you let Mr. Shorty out?"

"Of course." Her breath caught at how naturally he'd asked her to do something—him, who didn't ask people for things ever.

"We'll head to the kitchen, and I'll make us some breakfast."

"Not eggs," he groaned. "Please, no more eggs."

"Well, I don't know what else is in there," she pointed out. "Unless Lady Robinson's cook somehow left some meals? Which I highly doubt. Although we don't have that many eggs left. But it's either more eggs or we starve, I think."

"Unggh" was his only response as he drew his blanket up over his face.

"Come along, Mr. Shorty. Your master needs to de-grumpify."

She beckoned to the dog, who followed her down to the kitchen, where she looked around for not eggs while Mr. Shorty did his business.

Could they have cheese for breakfast? And what about Mr. Shorty? The dog trotted back in just as she was pondering his food. She filled the teakettle, then frowned at the unlit stove. Drat. And here she'd been feeling as though she could take care of herself and of him too.

Well. She'd just have to figure out how to light the stove. It had to be similar to a fire, right?

"Do you need help?"

She whirled around at the sound of his voice. "I do, only I didn't want to ask for it. But now that you're here, and you're less grumpy—you are less grumpy, right?"

He nodded, a wry grin lifting up one corner of his mouth. "I am, and I find I am hungry." He walked forward, and her stomach whooshed as he approached her, his eyes locked on hers. "But not for eggs."

She felt her breath catch as she realized she was just wearing her shift. And that his shirt was untucked and unbuttoned so she could see his neck and the top of his chest.

Dark hair curled out of his shirt, and she had the sudden urge to twine her fingers in it, see how it felt.

"What—what do you want?" Her voice sounded breathy. No wonder, given what his intense gaze was doing to her breath.

"A kiss, Pearl." He stood in front of her, close but not touching her. As though he was waiting for her response.

Was his consideration because he knew he was so imposing? Or was it because he was still unsure of her reaction?

No matter what it was, it was lovely.

"I can oblige you then," she replied, stepping forward so her breasts pressed against his chest. She tilted her face up and put her hands on his shoulders, raising herself up on tiptoe. He lowered his mouth to hers, gripping her waist.

Rough stubble rubbed against her skin as his warm mouth opened, his tongue licking at the seam of her lips. She gasped, opening for him, feeling her breasts against his solid chest, her nipples tightening from the friction.

His hand moved to her hip, caressing the curve there, then slid slowly down until his palm was on her arse. He squeezed it in his hand, and she shuddered in response.

"Is this all right?" he murmured against her mouth.

Still being considerate, even as she was close to forgetting her own name.

"Mmm-hmm," she said. She put her hands against his waist, then slid her fingers underneath his shirt, feeling his warm skin.

He put his other hand on her arse and raised her up, one big palm picking up her leg and wrapping it around his body, then doing the same to the other leg so she was pressed up against him, his hands holding her up.

It was intoxicating feeling how strong he was. As though he could support her no matter what.

The position meant that her female parts were pressed up against him also, and the sensation was wickedly pleasurable. She couldn't resist shifting so she could rub herself on his body.

"God, Pearl," he groaned, then swung her around to lay her gently down on the kitchen table. Thankfully there was nothing on it. "You look good enough to eat," he said, his gaze raking her from head to toe. She forgot to be self-conscious under his scrutiny because his expression was so . . . *hungry*.

"This table isn't big enough for both of us," she said, sitting up. "Let's go back to where we slept. Our breakfast can wait."

She hopped off the table and held her hand out. He took it, and she began to walk back to their room, slowing her pace because of his injury.

She was conscious that he could likely see the shape of her body through her shift, but she didn't mind. She just wished he was wearing something just as flimsy as she was—she wanted to see him as much as she believed he wanted to see her.

"Are you certain, Pearl?"

His voice was ragged, and she smiled, a wicked smile that he could not see.

"I am." She turned around to face him, stepping forward to gaze up into his eyes. She felt the focus of his attention as though it were a physical caress, and she shivered in response.

"Are you cold?" he said, his eyebrows furrowing in apparent concern.

She shook her head, never dropping her gaze. "I feel as if I am burning up," she replied, turning back around. "Perhaps that is because it is you *stoking my fire*." She said the last bit in an exaggerated tone, and she heard him snort in response.

Not quite what you want to hear during a romantic moment, but then again, it was she who had said the words in the first place. And if she could make him laugh, the most grumpy of grumpy earls?

It was too rare an opportunity to pass up.

"You'll pardon me if I bellows too much," he replied, emphasizing "bellows" to ensure she got the joke.

"You are lighting me up with your humor," she shot back, relishing his quick laugh.

They had reached the room, and she felt her stomach wobble a bit. Did she want to continue this? Was it part of her adventure or a foolhardy escapade?

And was there truly a difference?

"Are you all right?" he asked in a concerned tone. He reached up to cup her face in his warm hands. "I would ask if the flames of your desire have ebbed, but I don't want to make light of the situation."

"You do realize you made two puns in that last bit, don't you?" she asked, feeling her discomfort ease. Even though they'd only known each other for a few days—even though it felt like forever—she trusted him. This was the natural and perfect consequence of their being together like this.

"Let me make you groan in a different way," he said, his words soft, but the sexual impact hitting her hard.

"Only if you promise not to stop until we're both well and truly heated," she said. His eyes lit up as though she had started a fire within him. Which, she supposed, she had.

"God, yes," he said before crashing his mouth down on hers, his hands seeming as if they were on every part of her body.

He kissed her so intensely it was as though she could hear it, a rhythmic hammering that might have been her heart, or his, or—

"The door!" she exclaimed, leaping back, her eyes wide.

"Ignore it, they'll go away," he replied, pulling her back into his arms and lowering his mouth to her neck, making her arch in response.

The knocking continued.

And then they heard voices.

"Owen! Open the door, we know you're in there."

Chapter Ten

On the tenth day of Christmas
my true love gave to me
Ten unwelcome people wanting to see (me)

His mother.

"Owen, we're outside, and Nesta is in need of the facilities."

And his sister.

"Owen." Now it was Gwyneth's voice, which meant that Bryn was out there too.

All four of the women in his family were outside demanding to be let in. Whereas the only place he wanted to be let in was—well. He couldn't think about that, not with all of his relatives outside.

Mr. Shorty began to bark excitedly, running down the hall into the room.

"It's your family?" Pearl said, gasping. She leapt into action, grabbing her gown at the end of the sofa, tossing it over her head as she began to do something to her hair. "Button me."

"Owen!" His mother sounded exasperated. "We can hear your dog, we know you have to be in there. Unless you're unable to come to the door?"

"Owen, are you incapacitated?" Bryn's worried voice made him wince.

"I have to get the door," he said, glancing over his shoulder to where the thumping was getting louder. Mr. Shorty barked more insistently.

"I'll go to the kitchen, you make an excuse, and come find me so you can do me up," she said in a sputter.

She hurried out of the room, holding her gown up at the back with one hand, the other at her skirts, her hair tumbling down her back.

He walked as quickly as he was able to once she was safely out of sight, piling all of their linens together so it looked like a makeshift dog bed. Hopefully.

At least he didn't have to worry about appearing inappropriate in front of his family—his mother's voice at the door had ensured that had been taken care of.

He swung the door open, Mr. Shorty yipping happily beside him.

"Finally," his mother said, sweeping into the hallway. "We were about to find someone to break down the door, Bryn was certain you had tripped and knocked yourself unconscious."

"Because there would be no other reason you would possibly not want to open the door," his youngest sister Nesta murmured, accompanying her words with a rueful eye roll.

"Why are you here, Mam?" Owen said, addressing his mother.

His mother's expression was aghast. "Not come to see my only son at Christmas? Leaving him to the wilds of London injured and alone?"

His mother always did have a flair for the dramatic.

"London is not wild, Mam," Bryn corrected. "It is just filled with Londoners. Not the same thing."

"There was no need," Owen replied, trying not to grit his teeth. They never understood his need to be alone—not even Nesta, who was closest to him.

"There was every need," Gwyneth replied, her imperious tone making his jaw clench. "Robert had business in the city, so I suggested he take care of it now during Christmas so we could all be together."

Wonderful. His mother, his sisters, and his brother-in-law, who made his rigid sister Gwyneth seem like a free spirit.

"Aren't you going to invite us in?" his mother said as she walked down the hall toward the room he'd just been in. "We're thirsty, we could all use some tea," she called.

"It seems as though there is no need for me to invite you in," Owen murmured. Nesta caught his words and grinned in reply. "I'll just go and take care of finding some tea," Owen said in a louder voice.

"We'll just get settled," Gwyneth replied, following their mother down the hall.

Bryn did the same as Nesta took his arm and squeezed it. "I tried to dissuade them, but they were set on it. Mam started talking about you being alone at Christmas, and then Gwyneth got this trip into her head and . . ." Her words trailed off as she shook her head.

"I know." Owen patted Nesta's hand. "Go on with them, I'll be back in a moment."

"It'll only be for a bit tonight and then Christmas Day," Nesta continued. "Robert booked rooms for us at Grillon's."

Oh thank God. He hadn't even considered that they might want to stay the night.

Because if they did—oh hell, the kitchen! Pearl in there half-dressed as he dealt with his family.

"I'll be right back with tea," he said, snatching his cane up from the corner of the room and walking as swiftly as he could down the hall to the kitchen.

She'd managed to do up about half the buttons by the time he entered.

He looked pained, and she wished there was something she could do to help. Though she had been trying that, hadn't she, before they arrived? And it wouldn't be suitable to continue that activity now, not with his entire family in residence.

"They're all here," he muttered as she presented her back to him. She sighed as she felt his fingers on her skin. "My mother, all three of my sisters, and my brother-in-law. Well, he is off doing business somewhere, but he is in London as well." She felt him shake his head. "The only thing I wanted for Christmas was to be left alone. And here they are."

"At least they noticed you were gone." She tried not to sound mournful, but honestly, it was difficult not to.

"I know you're here," he replied in a low tone. He brushed

his lips at the nape of her neck, and she shivered. "You are all I want. Perhaps tied up with one of those ribbons." His voice had lowered, sounding all dark and full of passion.

Oh. That was an intriguing image, the thought of him undoing her—both figuratively and literally—making her body heat.

"Thank you." She turned to face him as he patted the top of her gown, indicating she was buttoned up. "But you should be grateful they care for you so deeply."

He made a derisive noise in response.

"They don't care for you?" She gestured toward where she presumed they were. "But they're here. They traveled a long distance to ensure you weren't alone for Christmas."

"Owen, you got a tree! I certainly didn't expect—" One of Owen's sisters entered the kitchen at a brisk pace, catching herself up short when she saw Pearl.

"Oh goodness. Well." And she glanced at Owen, and then back at Pearl, her face slowly turning red. "If we'd known you had . . . *company*," she said in a stiff tone of voice, "we certainly would not have—"

"Lady Pearl, might I introduce my sister Bryn, soon to be Mrs. Davies?" Pearl had never heard him sound so authoritative. There was something thrillingly attractive about how firmly he spoke. "Bryn, this is Lady Pearl Howlett, she and her parents, the Duke and Duchess of Marymount, live next door. Lady Pearl has been helping me walk Mr. Shorty during my convalescence." Thus neatly explaining why she was in the house with him alone.

Pearl watched as Owen's sister reassessed her first

impression, given the new information Owen made certain she knew. Bryn shared Owen's dark hair, but her eyes were lighter, and of course she wasn't nearly as broad. Her dark blue gown was both practical and fashionable, and looked to be very warm as well. Made with wool from his sheep?

"It is a pleasure to make your acquaintance, my lady," Mrs. Davies replied. "And thank you for helping my brother in his time of need."

I haven't helped him nearly enough. If you hadn't arrived, I'd be helping him this very moment. And he me. She smothered a grin at the thought, and caught Owen's eyes, nearly bursting out in laughter at his expression—as though he had thought the same thing, and was both irritated and abashed at his sister's words.

"Your brother has repaid whatever kindness I've given him by assisting me." Pearl responded without thinking, and then wanted to hit herself in the head for her words. How had he assisted her? Why did he have to anyway?

"Assisting Lady Pearl by accompanying her shopping. It is her doing that I have a Christmas tree," Owen interjected.

Bravo, she wished she could say. Another excellent rescue.

Of course, it made sense he would be a quick thinker around his family. It was probably so he could preserve some of his own time, since he'd said his family viewed him as someone who did things for them, not someone to care for.

That made her sad, but she was grateful at the moment for the result.

"I should be returning home," Pearl said. "I plan on

sitting in front of the fire this evening, perhaps stoking it if it gets too low."

Owen made a strangled noise in his throat, and she suppressed a smile. What was the point of behaving dangerously if you didn't tempt possible exposure?

"I will collect your cloak, my lady," he said. He walked out of the room, glancing back with a pained expression. Pained because he was leaving her? Because he didn't want his family here? Or pained because he wanted to continue what they'd been doing? Or was it because he'd woken from the dream of the last few days and knew that what they were about to do was wrong?

Drat. She hoped it wasn't that last one. His adventure might have been curtailed by his family's arrival, but hers hadn't been.

Although she would have to reconfigure what it was she wanted from her adventure, if he wasn't going to be part of it.

Being alone without him was much less appealing now. She wasn't quite to the point where she'd welcome her mother's return, but she was more willing to be rescued than she had been an hour ago.

"I hope you have a pleasant visit, Mrs. Davies," Pearl said. "Lord—" and then she paused, realizing she didn't remember his full name, just that he was an earl. She waved her hand, as though interrupting her own thought. "That is, it is very good of you to come all this way to visit your brother."

Mrs. Davies nodded, a look of smug satisfaction on her face. "Yes, well, it was managed with some difficulty. But we would not have Owen be alone during Christmas, he would hate that."

You don't know him at all, do you?

"And we were hoping he could show us around London."

Oh. You came here to see your recovering brother so he could guide you around a city he doesn't care for with an injured leg?

Perhaps that was harsh, but it was clear that Owen's family were not here for purely altruistic reasons.

Humph. Now she wanted even more to do something purely for him.

But that might be just as selfish as his family—making oneself feel better by doing a good turn.

Although if they did something they both enjoyed . . .

She felt her face grow hot, and hoped it wasn't noticeable. And where was Owen with her cloak anyway?

"I will just go find my cloak. Your brother probably was detained in his return." *By a member of your family who wanted something.*

Humph again.

She strode down the hallway, wishing there was a way to let him know she understood better how he felt—it was likely as onerous to be the focus of a family's attention as it was disheartening to be forgotten.

She nearly bumped into him in the dark hall, but his hands shot out to clasp her arms so she remained steady.

"Pearl," he said in a whisper. "I apologize for—"

"For what?" she replied back in the same quiet tone. "It isn't as though you knew they were coming."

"No. I just don't want them to suspect—"

"That we were engaged in fire-stoking activities?"

He chuckled, as she'd hoped he would. She'd come to realize, in the short time she'd known him, that Owen took things far too seriously. He needed to allow himself to have fun. Which was why it was so lovely to spend time with him, to watch him grow more relaxed.

Not to mention he was an excellent kisser.

"Will you be all right? On your own?"

It was sweet, his being worried about her. And necessary, she had to admit. She had no food, and she had only the most rudimentary knowledge about how to build a fire.

"I will be fine, I promise." If she had to go out to find food and warmth, she would. She could take care of herself, even if initially she'd been a bit flummoxed.

"I will come over after dinner," he said.

She hesitated before replying. She didn't want him to feel obliged, but she also wanted him to visit.

"You can if you truly wish to," she said in an earnest tone. "But you are under no obligation to me, I promise."

His hands tightened on her arms. "I want to. Dinner will be enjoyable, because I do care for my family. But it is a duty. Spending time with you is a pleasure I find I do not want to deprive myself of."

"Well, when you phrase it that way," she said teasingly, raising herself up to press her mouth against his.

He immediately drew her closer into his body, and she shivered in delicious reaction.

"I will see you later," he said. "I want to spend Christmas Eve with you."

His words sent a warmth through Pearl, one she'd never experienced before. Likely because nobody had ever wanted to be just with her—her sisters loved her, and she shared a close bond with her twin, but they took her presence for granted. None of them had ever specifically requested her company.

But he had.

"I can't wait," she said, then darted past him, trying to keep her steps as silent as possible so she could slip out.

Chapter Eleven

On the eleventh day of Christmas
my true love gave to me
The most special evening that ever could be

Pearl was sitting cross-legged on the floor facing the fireplace, admiring her handiwork, when she heard the door open. She immediately unfolded herself and stood, then tore down the hall to where Owen had just stepped in. He'd only walked the few feet from his house to hers, and yet his dark hair was covered with snow, as were his shoulders.

She began to brush him off as he removed his coat, stomping his feet to rid them of the snow.

"Dinner didn't seem to take long," she remarked, glancing at the clock that still wasn't telling the time. She had no idea how to wind the clock, and she didn't want to be conscious of time passing anyway, since it would mean that the adventure would be that much closer to ending.

"Gwyn's husband had to get up early for some very important business meeting," he said in a dry tone, indicating how important he viewed the meeting. "At least it meant I wouldn't have to hear about how he was the only possible person who could negotiate this particular deal."

"Kind of a boor, your sister's husband?"

He rolled his eyes. "You have no idea."

She grinned. "Oh, but I do. My sister Ida has a penchant for starting conversations that absolutely nobody in her vicinity wishes to hear. I love her, and I respect her intelligence, but I don't always want to know the particulars of each scientific discovery from ancient times."

He snorted. "I can see that."

"What about Mr. Shorty?"

He raised an eyebrow. "Sometimes I wonder if you like me or my dog more."

She crossed her arms over her chest. "Sometimes I do too," she replied with a smirk. "But Mr. Shorty doesn't know how to make eggs, or ask me about myself, or undo my gown. I definitely don't think he likes puns as much as you do."

"That's because it's a dog's life," he replied in an exaggeratedly mournful tone. Then he spoke more naturally. "Mr. Shorty is fine. I left him with a bone and he won't need to go out again until mid-morning, at least. He has gotten accustomed to your leisurely London ways."

"Excellent," she replied, relieved. If irked—"Leisurely London ways?" she repeated. He opened his mouth to respond, but she waved her hand. They only had one night, one Christmas Eve. She didn't want to spend it hearing about his diligent Welsh ways. Except in the ways that mattered. "Never mind that. Come into the salon, I have stoked the fire."

"You started without me," he said, the nuance in his words sending a flush to her cheeks.

"Not *that* fire. I wouldn't know how to start by myself."

"I'd like to see it if you did, Pearl." He took her hand as he spoke, brushing his fingers against hers. The touch sent skitters of awareness through her whole body.

"I'd like you to show me, Owen."

She heard his sudden intake of breath and allowed a small smile to cross her lips. She liked rattling him. She liked being so important to him, even for the short time of their adventure, that whatever she said would cause a reaction.

She would miss being the focus of someone's attention when their adventure ended.

But she couldn't look forward to that, or else she'd be glum. This, the now, the present, was what was important.

They entered the salon, and she glanced from the blazing fire to his face, which held an admiring expression.

"Excellent work. I don't think you need my help stoking any longer."

She raised her brow and gave him a knowing look.

"At least that kind of stoking," he added. He tilted his chin toward the sofa. "Go lie on that."

She gave him a skeptical look. "In my gown?"

"There will be time to remove that. I want to see you bare, stripped of all the things that aren't truly Pearl. But first I want to watch you stoke." Ooh. She felt all shivery when he used that commanding voice.

"What would those things be?" she asked, walking to the sofa and lying back against the sofa's arm. Her legs were stretched out on the cushions, the hem of her gown halfway up so it showed her feet, ankles, and shins. Tonight she hadn't worn stockings, since she much preferred bare feet.

She hoped he did too.

He approached her, undoing his neckcloth as he walked, his gaze focused intently on her face. He bit his lip for a moment, and Pearl responded so viscerally to that image it felt as though he had bitten her—and she liked it.

"Mm," she murmured, surprised to hear the noise emerge from deep inside.

By now, he had removed his coat and was just in his shirt, rolling up the sleeves to reveal his strong forearms. She'd seen forearms before, of course, she wasn't that sheltered of a duke's daughter, but she had never felt as strong a reaction to seeing a body part that was sometimes visible.

How would she react when she saw a body part that wasn't commonly visible? Not just *that*, but also his chest, his back, his legs, and those strong shoulders.

"Pearl, you are so lovely." He spoke the words in a hush, and his sincerity warmed her throughout her entire body. "I don't know that I would think you so lovely if I didn't appreciate you." His face fell. "Wait. Was that not a compliment? I find you beautiful, Pearl." He looked abashed, and Pearl rushed to reassure him, raising herself up off the sofa to kneel on the cushions and reach for his face.

"It's the best compliment I have ever received." She smirked as she caught his eye. "Since mostly the compliments I get are that I am not as obnoxious as my sister, not as pedantic as another, and not as poor-sighted as yet another." She tilted her head as she sat back down. "So I have replied to your sort of compliment with something equally hamstrung."

"It seems we are perfect for one another."

And then they both froze. They had not discussed this beyond this moment.

Did he mean—?

"Do you mean—?" she began, only to stop as he suddenly knelt on the floor, placing his large, warm palms on her shins and beginning to slide them up to her knees and down to her ankles.

"No stockings," he murmured. "I like feeling your bare skin, Pearl. I like feeling you."

"I like you feeling me as well," Pearl replied, not surprised to hear how breathy she sounded. Since she could feel her breath hitching in her chest. Her entire focus was on his fingers, stroking her skin, stopping right where her gown began.

She tugged at the fabric, raising the gown up over her knees and to her hips, just barely covering there where she was entirely naked.

"Pearl." He spoke in a serious tone as his fingers trembled against her skin. "Are you certain?"

She raised her head and met his gaze. "This is my adventure, Owen. I want to have it. All of it. I want to have you."

His eyelids lowered, and she saw an intensity in his expression she hadn't seen before. An expression that promised she would definitely have all the adventure she craved.

"I'm going to slide my hands on your legs. Tell me if you wish me to stop."

He took a deep breath, and began the excruciatingly slow slide up her shins, over her knees, onto her thighs until his fingers were just barely inside the crook of her thigh. So close to that spot, the one that throbbed.

"Touch me," she said.

One corner of his mouth tilted up and he met her gaze. "I want you to touch yourself, Pearl. Show me how you want to be touched."

Her cheeks grew immediately hot, and she felt herself start to prickle all over. "Touch myself?" She sounded curious, but unsure.

"Where do you ache, Pearl?" he asked, moving his fingers a tiny bit closer to there.

She swallowed. "You know where."

"Show me."

Still keeping her eyes on his, she reached down and plucked the fabric of her gown so it rested on her hips, revealing her most private place. He didn't look down there, however, at least not right away, which made her more confident of her next actions.

She placed one finger on top, right where she burned, and immediately groaned. He clenched his jaw and made a strangled noise deep in his throat. His fingers grew tighter on her thighs. She'd have marks after. A tangible reminder of this adventure.

"And—?" he urged. "What is it you want to do? Tell me. I need to hear you tell me, Pearl."

The need in his voice was palpable. "I want to put two fingers there," she said, suiting her actions to her words. "I want to rub that spot with my two fingers. It feels as though I need to touch that spot." She moistened her lips. "And I want you to touch my breasts while I touch myself."

He didn't reply, but got up to walk to the end of the sofa, pushing on her shoulders so she scooted down the couch, her gown ruching up even higher. He slid in behind her, drawing her to lie against his chest, wrapping his arms around her, his palms resting flat on her belly.

Owen was so hard it was painful. Her desire for an adventure, her desire for him, was far more alluring than anything his imagination had ever conjured. His cock throbbed with the need to be inside her, but he reminded himself to be patient. Just like shearing a sheep, one had to be thorough to get all the wool.

Not the metaphor anybody else would have thought of, of course. And rather awkward, come to think about it.

He needed to stop thinking about it. And just do.

He began to slide his palm toward her breast. He could feel her breath coming short and fast. And then she put her hand on his and dragged it swiftly on top of her full roundness, pushing his hand into the soft flesh. "They're aching to be touched, Owen. Touch me."

He squeezed her, and then his index finger found her nipple, dragging his fingertip back and forth across the taut peak.

"Don't forget to keep your end of the bargain," he said, nodding toward where her hands lay on her thighs. "Touch your pretty pussy for me, Pearl. Show me what it looks like when you climax."

Her breath shuddered, and he held his own, wondering if he had gone too far, had frightened her somehow.

"I might just climax if you keep talking to me like that," she said in a low, sensual voice. "It feels so good. Me leaning against you, feeling how . . . excited you are, you touching me as I touch myself."

So she wasn't scared. She was excited. He couldn't resist pressing his iron-hard cock a little harder in a vain attempt to ease his own ache.

"We'll have to do something about that later," she said, her words sounding like a promise.

"How does it feel, Pearl? When you rub your fingers?"

She arched her back so that her face was beside his. "It feels wonderful. As though there is something to be finished, some sort of urgency to the action, but all of the action is pleasurable."

"And when I touch your pretty breasts? Not that I know that they are pretty, but I am assuming so, since they are yours."

"Do you want to see?"

Owen's cock twitched. "I do. More than you could possibly imagine. But I want to see you claim your pleasure first."

"Oooh," she moaned. The rhythm of her fingers was growing faster. Owen pinched her nipple, then petted it. "Owen, is it supposed to feel this good?"

"Yes." He couldn't keep his eyes from down there, where

her fingers were rubbing and stroking, her hips shifting in response.

And then—"Ooooh!" she cried out as she shook against him, her eyes closed, her lips parted.

He'd never seen anything so lovely in his life.

He kept his palms on her breasts, feeling how her chest was rising and falling rapidly as she breathed.

"My goodness," she said at last, turning to look at him with a sated expression. "That was incredible."

"It was. And I am honored to see it. I didn't know I would be receiving this rare and gorgeous a Christmas gift. To see your passion."

"And yours?" she said, twisting her body to press her side against his chest. She placed her hand on his trousers, just on top of his cock, and trailed her fingers up and down his rigidity. "You'll tell me if I'm doing this wrong?"

"You couldn't do it wrong," he replied. "There's no wrong when it comes to pleasure, Pearl. If it doesn't feel as good as something else could, I'll tell you. But there are no wrongs here. Not between us, not now."

"Oh," she replied on a sigh. "Can I—?" And she put her palm on the placket of his trousers. "I want to touch it. Directly."

Owen had never wanted his trousers off as much as he did now. He pushed himself up off the sofa as she undid his trouser fall, and then she slid them off so they were tangled about his ankles. He wriggled his feet to get them entirely off, then flung the trousers onto the floor.

"Oh, your legs," she said in a hushed tone.

Right. He'd forgotten about the injury, which was still an angry red bruise on his left knee. "I'm sorry, I should have warned you."

"Warned me about what? How strong and gorgeous your legs are?"

"No, the aftermath of the groundhog incident. It's ugly."

"It's not ugly," she retorted. "It is the reason you are here in London in the first place, so I cannot dislike it. I am grateful to it. And to that groundhog."

"Don't go too far. That groundhog deserves nothing more than banishment."

"Fine. The groundhog is culpable." Her tone was laughing. "But your legs truly are gorgeous, Owen. All muscular and strong and hairy."

"I have to admit that doesn't sound gorgeous to me."

"That's because you're not me," she asserted. "But meanwhile, I have something I wanted to see. Can I?" she asked, sliding her hand down his belly toward where his shaft was tenting his smallclothes. "I didn't realize you wore all those things on the bottom half."

He took his smallclothes off just as speedily as he had his trousers, tossing them onto the floor as well. He would not spend time pondering how ridiculous he looked, a shirt on his upper half, nothing on his lower half, lying on a sofa that barely fit his height.

And then could not spend time pondering anything at all, since she curled her hand into a fist around his cock and began to slide it up and down.

"God, Pearl," he groaned.

"I take it this is not wrong?" she said, a wry tone to her voice.

"You are correct."

He put his palm over hers and demonstrated how to work him best, then let go so she could keep stroking his penis.

And then he felt the start of his climax as it started to build from somewhere down in the soles of his feet, up through his legs, spreading throughout his entire body until he groaned and ejaculated onto his lower belly, narrowly missing her legs and the sofa.

He lay panting in the immediate aftermath as she petted his chest underneath his shirt. "That was tremendous," he said after a while.

"Good, because I didn't manage to purchase you anything for Christmas," she shot back in a cheeky voice.

He cleaned off the mess with his shirt, then dumped it on a pile on the floor.

"Vixen," he said, rolling over to gather her into his arms, then carefully picking her up to deposit her directly in front of the fireplace.

"I am hardly a vixen," she said demurely, but her eyes were humorous.

"You're my vixen," he replied, burying his nose in the tendrils of her hair. He wished he could stay lost like this forever. Long past Christmas, when the days were just filled with January gray, when he was walking normally again, but his heart now held a bruise.

He didn't want this adventure to end, that was for certain. But he didn't know how she felt about it, and he didn't want to force her into something that she didn't want.

She'd tell you if she didn't want it, a voice reminded him. But if her family discovered what had happened, she'd be forced into it. And the only way for them not to find out about it was for them to seem to be complete strangers, as though they'd never met.

It was unlikely that his sisters, buried in Wales as they were, would ever come into contact with anybody who would know her. A secret part of him wished they would, so he could get what he wanted, which was her. But that would be as unfair to her as it was for his family to constantly pressure him about marriage—something he was going to have a discussion with them about soon.

"What are you thinking about?" she asked in a hesitant tone. "You've been making all kinds of noises, and not all of them seem as though they are blissful ones."

He kissed her hair, then drew back to stare into her face. "Just thinking about how perfect this has been. I have had a Christmas I will remember for the rest of my life." He could feel the pain beginning, a slow ache just below his heart, constricting his breath and making his life seem that much duller. Without her.

"I have too. And it's all due to you. And Mr. Shorty, of course." She smiled at him, then placed a soft kiss on his lips. "Is there—is there more we could do?"

He shook his head, filled with more regret than he'd ever had in his life. "Not without running certain risks, which

I won't subject you to." Besides which, he wasn't certain he would be up to the task so quickly, given what a tremendous climax he'd had. But he wouldn't share that with her.

"We should curl in and go to sleep. Tomorrow it's Christmas Day!" she exclaimed.

"I've already gotten my Christmas present," he said in a soft voice, squeezing her tightly.

She smiled up at him, nodding her head. "Me too. I lo—I am so glad you were part of my adventure. Even if I didn't get hot chocolate after all."

What had she been about to say? Was it the same thing he wanted to say to her? And what would it mean if they admitted it?

He'd have to think it through. Would he dare to ask her to leave London, a place she seemed to know and like, for a remote sheep farm in Wales where she'd be living with his mother and his as yet unmarried sisters?

Would this magical dream of their not-so-instant connection fade away when faced with the reality of everyday life?

He knew it wouldn't for him. With her, he could be himself: someone who loved puns and doing work not normally done by an earl. She wouldn't ask what he could do for her, but would insist upon doing things for him.

He'd known her for what, two or three days, and already he knew she was the wife for him.

But he wouldn't demand that her adventure turn into the rest of her life. Not without her wanting that too.

He just had to figure out how to ask that.

Chapter Twelve

On the twelfth day of Christmas
my true love gave to me
Twelve words that delighted me

Goodness. That interlude was certainly enlightening. Her body still pulsed with the aftereffects of pleasure, and she felt her cheeks heat at recalling what they'd done.

It was early, so early the dawn had barely just begun. She glanced over at the window, which revealed a clear sky. The snow must have stopped then.

Which meant her adventure was nearly over.

She rolled over, flinging her hand out to touch him.

But he wasn't there.

And she felt her heart sink. Had he slunk off because she'd embarrassed herself?

No, he was just as pleased as she was at what had happened.

Had he left to check on Mr. Shorty?

No, because he'd specifically mentioned that Mr. Shorty wouldn't need to go out until hours from now.

Because he didn't want to be caught. Because he didn't

want to be forced into marriage with her, despite what had happened between them.

"Well," she said in a determined voice, "I didn't want that either. We told one another this was only an interlude. An adventure." Which was also why he hadn't pressed the opportunity to thoroughly compromise her.

It was all so clear. And she knew that, she had said it herself, for goodness' sake! But there had been a part of her that had secretly wondered if he might want to make this interlude permanent.

But she had to forget that silly idea. It was Christmas morning, her mother would be coming to fetch her soon, and she'd return to being the *not* sister.

And he had seen her, for a time.

She pulled on her gown, twisting it to do up the buttons at the bottom before stretching her arms to take care of the ones at the top. There were only a few in between she couldn't reach. She wouldn't have even thought of trying before all this started, so at least something good had happened.

Plus she had met him. And he had given her food, and warmth, and companionship, and passion.

What else could she possibly want?

She would be fine. She would.

She roused herself at the sound of knocking on the door, her heart immediately racing to imagine it was him.

Likely it was her mother. Not him.

But when she opened the door, it *was* him. And he looked as awkward and uncomfortable and nearly grumpy as when she had first met him.

"Good morning, my lady," he said, glancing behind him.

Some of his family were behind him, placing various packages into a large coach.

"You're going."

"No. I mean, yes, but—"

"Thank you for coming to say good-bye," she interrupted, the sting of tears in her eyes.

"I didn't—"

"Well, then," she said, beginning to shut the door.

He stuck his foot in to prevent her closing it. "Wait a minute. I haven't said what I came to say." He pulled something out of his waistcoat pocket. "I have something for you. If you want it."

It was the dragon ornament.

"But that's yours. That's from your father, you can't give it to me."

"I want to." He pointed to where the eye had been missing. In its place was a tiny perfect pearl. It didn't match the other eye, of course, but it was there. "I want you to have it, no matter what."

She gave him a confused look. "No matter—?"

"What if I don't want to go back?" he blurted.

Pearl's eyes widened. "What, you want to stay here?"

He took a deep breath. "I want to stay with *you*. Forever, if you'll agree to it."

"What?" Her eyes got even wider.

"Pearl, I don't want to force you into anything you don't want to do. It's clear what your mother wants for you, from what you've said. And my mother wants the same thing for me. But these past few days I've—I've never felt so relaxed. Do you know how it feels for me to be able to say what I want without constantly thinking about how the person hearing it will react? If I say, 'I don't feel well,' to immediately hear how that means I won't be able to do something for somebody? You don't want me to do anything for you."

She opened her mouth to retort that there were things, thank you very much, but she didn't even have to speak the words before he was chuckling in response.

"Well, except for that, which I will gladly do.

"But I want you to consider, after the magic of Christmas is over, and our tree has gone up in smoke when one of our queen's beloved candles has set off the conflagration, that we might belong together. That I think we belong together because—" and she saw him take a deep breath and swallow "—because I think I might be falling in love with you." He gestured to the ornament. "I put a pearl in the dragon's eye because you I want you to be a part of my life. My memories. My *home*."

Oh.

"Oh," she breathed.

"And I don't want you to answer right away, since that wouldn't be fair to you." His expression made it seem as though he were anxious she were going to say no anyway.

"But if after a month or so you discover you feel the same way about me, I want to know so I can propose. I'm deliberately not proposing now because that would put you on the spot, and that's not fair."

"But—" *But what if I want to hear the words?* But that would be forcing him as much as he didn't want to force her.

It was unfortunate they were both such considerate people.

"Just consider it," he said hastily. His cheeks were reddened, as though he was embarrassed. It was adorable, though she doubted anyone had called the Large Grumpy (but not really) Welsh Earl "adorable" before.

"Owen!" his mother called. "We have to be going."

"You're going." And he was taking her heart with him, and she couldn't tell him, because this was the worst possible time, and his mother was even now walking toward them, an impatient expression on her face.

Just give me a moment, Pearl pleaded in her head. *Just realize that your son's needs and wants come first, and he needs and wants me.*

But the woman didn't slow her pace.

"Lady Pearl, happy Christmas! I am delighted to get the chance to say good-bye."

"Good—" Pearl began, only to stop when another carriage pulled up. And then she groaned.

"Pearl! Pearl, thank God you're all right!"

Her mother.

The carriage stopped, and her mother flung herself out, pelting up the steps with far more energy than Pearl knew she had. Her sister Eleanor followed, walking more slowly, a rueful expression on her face. One Pearl knew well—Eleanor had just spent time alone in a carriage with their mother after all.

The duchess drew up as she spotted Owen, however, and she got that smug look on her face that made Pearl want to groan again.

"And who is this?" she said in a sly tone.

"That is my son, Owen Dwyfor, Earl of Llanover," Owen's mother replied stiffly. "And you are?"

"This is my mother, the Duchess of Marymount," Pearl supplied hastily. She hoped the ladies wouldn't get into some sort of Aristocracy One-upsmanship contest.

"Oh!" Owen's mother said in an entirely different tone of voice. "Well, that is lovely. We were about to leave, but surely we can stay for a bit? I know Owen wishes to say good-bye to Lady Pearl."

"Good-bye?" Pearl's mother said in disappointment.

Pearl rolled her eyes. *Thanks for making me seem pathetic, Mother.*

"Owen!" his mother called. "Come here and help with the luggage."

He gave her an exasperated look, but went to his mother as the duchess spoke.

"How could you leave us? And on Christmas too!"

"I believe you left me, Mother," Pearl replied. She glanced over her mother's shoulder to meet her sister Eleanor's sympathetic gaze.

"That doesn't matter," the duchess replied, waving her hand dismissively. "I am just grateful you haven't starved, or been eaten by dogs, or keeping company you should not have."

Those things are not the same, Pearl wanted to reply, but to her mother, they certainly were.

How would the duchess react to knowing that her last unmarried daughter had fallen in love with a Welshman?

Granted, he was an Earl, but the duchess would likely not recognize a Welsh title as being anywhere close to an English one.

"You're all right, Pearl?" Eleanor said, stepping forward to clasp Pearl's hand. She peered intently into her sister's face behind her spectacles. "Oh," she said after a moment. "You are all right." And then she smiled, a warm, knowing smile that told Pearl her sister had figured it out. Of course not the particulars, but that Pearl had fallen in love.

And at that moment, Pearl felt *seen*. It was lovely, to know her sister did care for her, even if she wasn't as bossy as Olivia, or as headstrong as Della, or as intelligent as Ida.

"Mother," Eleanor said in a louder voice, "I believe I left one of Ida's gifts here."

Even though both Pearl and Eleanor knew full well that Eleanor hadn't done any such thing.

Eleanor shot Pearl a conspiratorial smile. "Do what you need to do," she said in a whisper. "I'll distract her. That is, if you want?"

Pearl nodded vigorously. "I want. Thank you," she said.

She gave Eleanor a quick hug, then ran toward where Owen and his mother stood.

"Pardon me, my lord?"

He turned, giving her a look that nearly melted her. His eyes told her the truth of everything he'd just said—that he loved her, that he wanted her, that she fit. All this in just a few days. But she knew it was true, even if she had known him for years.

"Yes, my lady?"

She held her hand out. "I believe you have something of mine?"

He looked confused, then his expression cleared. "Oh. Yes." He dangled the ornament in the air between them, a hopeful look on his face.

"But I would like to place it on the tree that you bought."

He frowned, confused again. "Place it on—?"

"Yes. We will both be leaving soon, but I'd like the ornament to be where it belongs."

"Go on ahead, don't keep Lady Pearl waiting," Owen's mother said.

"Of course not." He dropped the ornament in Pearl's outstretched palm, then walked beside her up to Lady Robinson's home.

"What are you doing?" he whispered.

"I'm doing what I want to do," she whispered back. "I'm having my adventure."

They walked into the house, then Pearl turned the lock in the front door and grinned at Owen. "They won't be able to get in. Not until it's too late."

His eyes widened, and then he returned her smile.

She took his hand and led him to the room they'd slept in.

"Pearl?" he asked questioningly, but he followed her lead into the room.

"First we have to return the ornament to where it belongs." She glanced at him. "I love that you put a pearl in it." Had anybody ever done something so Pearl-specific in their lives?

She knew the answer to *that* question.

"How did you manage it?"

"I found a place when I was out to dine with my family, I told the jeweler it was a Christmas present, and that it was extremely important it be done within the hour. And I gave him a generous fee."

"I love it," she said as she put it in the center of the tree. Not too close to the candles, of course.

They stood looking at it for a few moments. And then heard the knocking.

"Owen!"

"Pearl!"

Their mothers were shouting their names simultaneously.

Pearl grinned. "Should I take care of this?"

Owen bowed. "Please do."

She scurried out of the room and walked to the front door. "Hello?" she called.

"Are you all right?" the duchess said.

"Yes, we are. Owen and I are just exchanging Christmas gifts. Perhaps you should all go get some tea, we might be a while."

Pearl smothered a giggle as she heard the shocked gasps, quickly followed by smug noises of satisfaction.

"We'll be back later. Quite later," the duchess called.

She waited as she heard them retreating, their excited tones of voice telling her just what they both thought of this particular outcome.

Glad we could please you by pleasing ourselves, she thought.

She returned to the room, their room, where Owen waited.

"Sit down," she said, gesturing to the sofa.

He sat, looking up at her.

"You didn't propose earlier."

His mouth opened, and she leaned forward to place her fingers on his lips. "Shh. Let me speak for a moment."

He nodded.

"I want to give you a Christmas gift."

As she spoke, she took the skirts of her gown and raised them, then got onto his lap facing him, one knee on either side of his legs.

"Pearl?"

She smiled and took his face in her hands. "As far as I can tell, nobody has ever asked you what you want. Not in everyday life, and certainly not for Christmas. That was apparent earlier, when you said you wouldn't force anything on me. You didn't say what you wanted, you just ensured I was accommodated as much as possible with no consideration of your own needs. Even earlier," she said, feeling her cheeks flush, "you made certain my needs were met before yours. You are the most generous, giving person I have ever met. So I want to ask you, Owen. What do you want, what do you truly want, for Christmas?"

He took a deep breath, his gaze steady on her face.

"You."

She grinned in response. "That is what I was hoping you would say. And, if it's not too selfish, let me tell you what I want for Christmas: you."

He smiled, a genuine, warm smile that made her tremble.

"And now," she said in a sly tone, "let's make certain neither one of us can exchange their gifts."

She leaned forward to press her body against his as she spoke, and his strong arms came around her.

"I want you to get what you want, Owen," she whispered.

Owen felt something ease inside as she spoke. Although other things tensed, given that her breasts were against his chest and her delightful curves were resting on top of his cock.

"Are you certain, Pearl?" He couldn't help but tighten his grip on her, even though he would let her go, if that was what she wished. "Because we've only known each other a few days."

"You told me how you feel, Owen. I haven't told you how I feel. Can I do that?"

It was unusual for anyone to ask his permission for something—usually they told him what was going to happen, and it generally involved effort on his part.

"Please," he replied.

She responded by kissing his neck softly, twining her fingers in his hair. "We have only known each other for a few days, but you took time to know me, even within a few minutes of meeting me." She chuckled. "Granted, you were rather abrupt, but you asked if I needed help. That is your way, Owen. You are a kind, generous, giving person who has to give without expecting anything in return. And normally not getting it." She trailed kisses on his neck and on his ear, sending shudders of desire coursing through him. "I like how you wanted to get to know me, how you asked questions and showed me things even though you likely thought me a nuisance."

He slid his hands up and down her back, feeling the indent of her waist, the flare of her hips.

"You took care with me, Owen. At each point of our adventure, you asked if I was all right, you made certain I wasn't frightened or anxious or hungry."

"Even if there were too many eggs," he replied gruffly. She laughed.

"And I know already that I think I'm falling in love with you too. I don't want to wait a month. I've waited my whole life for you. I want you now. If you want me."

"I do," he said, exhaling as he spoke.

As soon as he'd spoken, he gathered her tightly in his arms and rose, then placed her on the floor and took her hand, leading her out of the room and into the main hall.

"Where are we going?" Pearl asked.

"Bedroom," he replied.

He began to walk up the stairs. His limp was much less noticeable now, Pearl observed. She followed, grinning like a fool.

She hadn't been upstairs yet, but she didn't spare a glance at any of the furnishings in the rooms they passed, just kept her gaze on his broad back, on his disheveled hair that curled around his collar.

He led her into a bedroom with a massive bed in the middle. She didn't wait, she leapt onto it and bounced, much as she had when she was younger.

He didn't join her, not right away. Keeping his gaze locked with hers, he tugged on his shirt, then drew it over his head, revealing his strong, muscled body.

Looking at his beautiful form made her want to touch and kiss him everywhere. She felt her breath grow faster, and she got onto her knees and pulled at the back of her gown, too impatient to do a proper unbuttoning. The fabric pulled apart with a satisfying tearing noise, and then she drew it up over her head and tossed it onto the floor, leaning back entirely naked on the bed.

His eyes were wide, drinking her in. His hands went to his trousers, and he leaned over, tugging his boots off and then shoving his trousers down off his legs, leaving him naked as well.

"Owen, you are a splendid sight," Pearl said in a pleased tone of voice.

"As you are." His voice was husky, and she shivered in anticipation. "You're certain about this?" he asked.

She rolled her eyes. "You might outdo my sister Ida in asking questions. Yes, I'm certain. Come here and compromise me."

He grinned, then got onto the bed, the mattress dipping under his weight. He crawled forward, caging her with his arms, his penis brushing against her lower belly.

And then he lowered his mouth to kiss her, and she nearly forgot to breathe. His tongue swept inside her mouth, and his hands seemed to be everywhere, on her shoulders, her neck, her breasts. His fingers caressed her nipple, and she arched her back, which pushed her belly more into him.

He broke the kiss to utter some sort of inarticulate growl, and she found herself growling back, which made him break into an unexpected laugh.

She grinned, then wriggled underneath him, sliding her hands to grasp his shaft.

He closed his eyes in response, and she stroked him, watching his expression grow more intense.

"So good," he murmured, and then he slid his hand between them, finding that place that ached for his touch.

"Mm," she said. "Touch me."

"That is something I will gladly do for you," he said, his tone wry.

He put the palm of his hand on her mound, causing a surprisingly sensual pressure, and his fingers began to rub. "So wet already," he said.

"Mm," she said again. She felt the pleasure building with each caress.

"Owen, I want you." She accompanied her words with a wiggle of her hips to make it clear what she was talking about.

"You're—"

"Shut up, Owen," she said. "I want you now."

"So bossy," he replied.

He gripped his penis, his hand covering hers, and brought it to her opening, rubbing the head against that throbbing place. She bit her lip and held her breath as he began to enter, so slowly she thought she might die.

It hurt for a moment, but the hurt was much less than the rising pleasure, and then he was inside, his body on top of hers, her legs wrapped around his hips.

"Are you all right?" Of course he had to ask again. But it was so sweet, to be so cared for.

"I am," she replied. She ran her hands up and down his back, onto his arse, relishing the strength and size of him.

At her words, he began to move, raising himself up on his elbows and drawing himself in and out of her, his expression one of concentration.

It felt delicious and delightful, to have all that power and strength focused on her, and she closed her eyes to block out anything that wasn't the feel of his body sliding into her.

His pace increased, and soon he was moving quickly, the impact of his thrusts making her slide up the bed.

It felt tremendous.

She bit her lip as he continued his steady movement, then held her breath as he froze and flung his head back, howling his pleasure in a loud roar.

And then collapsed on top of her, finally not asking if she was all right underneath his weight.

She smiled at the thought.

"Merry Christmas, Owen. I most definitely received the gift I wanted," she said after a few moments.

"Merry Christmas, Pearl. I got more than I could have ever expected. Thank you."

Epilogue

"And then she told us to go get tea!" The duchess addressed the small gathering with her usual flair, allowing very few others to get a word in edgewise.

The wedding was a quiet affair, as suited Pearl and Owen, even if the duchess was miffed she couldn't celebrate the success of having married off the last Howlett sister.

Pearl sat next to Owen at the wedding breakfast as their mothers detailed everything leading up to their unusual engagement.

His hand found hers under the table, and he ran his fingers over the large ring he'd insisted on buying, even though Pearl thought it was far too extravagant.

"It's Christmas and a wedding gift rolled in one," he'd said in response.

"Are you happy?" he murmured.

She glanced over at him, looking at his dark, handsome face, which Olivia said made him look exactly like one of the heroes from one of her salacious novels. To which Pearl had just smiled knowingly, making Olivia's eyes go wide and her mouth open with all sorts of questions. Of course.

"I am. Even though," she continued, gesturing at the plates in front of them, "we are eating eggs again."

He groaned. "At least it's eggs in a different style this time. If they had served fried eggs, I might have refused to marry you."

"Too late. We're already married," she replied in a cheeky tone.

"Yes, and I did compromise you," he said in a mock suffering tone.

"I think I compromised you," she retorted.

He laughed, and she joined him, squeezing his hand under the table. They burst out into more laughter as they both felt a nudge at their legs, realizing Mr. Shorty was making his hunger known.

Pearl reached over the table for a piece of roast beef, then snuck it under the table.

"You'll spoil him," Owen warned.

"I plan on spoiling you."

He took a deep breath. "I plan on letting you too. I love you, Pearl."

"And I love you." Another nudge under the table. "And Mr. Shorty."

They both grinned, and she leaned over for a kiss.

Keep reading for a sneak peek at

NEVER KISS A DUKE

the first book in Megan Frampton's new
The Hazards of Dukes series
Coming February 2020

Keep reading for a sneak peek at

NEVER KISS A DUKE

the first book in Megan Frampton's new
The Hazards of Dukes series
Coming February 2020

Chapter One

Everything Sebastian had ever known was a lie.

"You're saying I'm no longer the duke. That I am illegitimate. Do I have that right?" Sebastian Dutton, the Duke of Hasford, spoke in a clipped, sharp tone. A tone he normally reserved for one of his dogs caught gnawing on a shoe.

This was much bigger than footwear.

Sebastian sat across from the solicitor's desk, his cousin Thaddeus Dutton, the Earl of Kempthorne, sitting beside him. Unlike Sebastian, Thaddeus looked as though he'd been up for hours—crisp, alert, and attentive. Likely he had; Thaddeus took his duties in service to Her Majesty very seriously. He had wanted to join the army since he and Sebastian had first played tin soldiers together.

The solicitor visibly swallowed before he replied to Sebastian's terse statement.

"Yes. You do not have claim to being the Duke of Hasford."

He heard Thaddeus emit a gasp, which was the most demonstrative Thaddeus ever got—his gasp was equal to another person's dead faint.

Sebastian had gotten up at a ridiculous time to attend this appointment—normally he would have sent his secretary, but the note from the solicitor's office had strongly emphasized he should attend in person. So he'd roused himself before noon, grouchily drank his coffee, and tried to look somewhat awake as he approached the address indicated on the note.

The cousins were both tall, but there the resemblance ended; where Sebastian was fair haired and lean, with an easy smile and an even easier charm, Thaddeus was dark, from his hair to his eyes to his dark sense of right and wrong.

They were opposites, and the best of friends. Dubbed the Angel and the Devil by their friends and family, though there were disputes as to which was which. In appearance, Thaddeus was devilish, but it was Sebastian's attitude toward life that earned him the sobriquet.

You do not have claim to being the Duke of Hasford.

Had the floor dropped out from under him, or was that just how he felt? For the first time, he knew no amount of personal magnetism or supreme confidence would rescue him from the situation.

"So who am I?" Sebastian asked. His words were spoken through a clenched jaw.

"Mr. de Silva," the solicitor replied.

Mr. de Silva, the illegitimate son of a duke. "My mother's name."

"Yes," the solicitor confirmed. "Your mother and your father were not legitimately married, because British law states that a man may not marry the sister of his late wife.

And your mother was the late duchess's sister, not her cousin, as she'd told your father." The man cleared his throat. "It's all detailed in the letters she wrote aboard ship."

"Of course she lied," Sebastian said bitterly. He'd always known his mother to be a scheming, heartless creature; her treatment of Ana Maria, his older half sister, proved that. He hadn't known she'd also been a liar.

At least she was consistent in her behavior, he thought humorlessly.

He leaned forward to look at the proof, the seemingly innocuous papers that lay on the solicitor's desk. Yellow, faded, and ragged around the edges, they were proof positive that Sebastian's parents' marriage was illegal. He recognized his mother's handwriting. And her duplicity.

"Where did these come from?" Sebastian demanded. He couldn't succumb to the dark hole that was threatening to engulf him. He had to keep asking questions, to find out what happened so he could understand. If it was possible to make sense of it at all.

The solicitor placed his hands flat on his desk, spreading his fingers wide. "They were found in the duchess's vault box. That is, your late mother." Since she wasn't actually the duchess. "Letters she wrote, but apparently never mailed. We discovered them after the accident."

The carriage accident that took both his parents' lives.

"But that was over six months ago," Thaddeus pointed out. "How is it that these are just coming to light now?"

"It takes time to review all the paperwork after such an

event," the solicitor said in a defensive tone. "And we needed to translate the letters," he added.

"Why would your mother lie?" Thaddeus said, turning his intense stare toward Sebastian. "There was no practical reason to hide the relationship."

Thaddeus, ever practical. Always searching for the reason in things. Whereas Sebastian never searched, things just arrived. Like his title, wealth, standing in society, women, and friends.

It was astonishing how quickly one's entire world could be upended. All in the time it took for the solicitor to explain how the letters of Sebastian's mother detailed every last subterfuge.

"My mother was ambitious," Sebastian replied. Unable to keep the animosity from his tone. "She probably persuaded the late duchess that there was some reason to keep their relationship a secret—maybe it would have reflected badly on the family for a sister to act as a companion." He shrugged, as though it didn't matter. Of course it mattered. "The point is that I am not the duke." He raked his hands through his hair, anger coursing through his veins.

The position he'd been trained for since he had been born was not his. The estates, the responsibility, the money, the title, the position—all of it gone.

"Who is?" Thaddeus asked.

Sebastian raised one wry eyebrow as he waited for Thaddeus to figure it out. And supplied the information when it seemed his normally sharp cousin was not processing it. "You're the Duke of Hasford now, Thad."

Sebastian didn't think he had ever seen Thaddeus surprised before. The man was confoundingly strategic, always plotting his next move, anticipating events long before anybody else involved had thought of them. It was what had made him invaluable when they were growing up together—Sebastian usually thought up the mischief, Thaddeus planned out the event, and their friend Nash was there to quash any trouble.

But now Thaddeus looked as though he'd been hit in the head with a heavy object. Or a dukedom.

"That's not—I mean," Thad sputtered.

If Sebastian were feeling more inclined, he'd have to laugh at his cousin's expression and inability to speak in a complete sentence. But he was not inclined. He was furious. With his mother, with his feckless, foolish father, with his own expectations.

"It is." He tapped the papers in front of them. "This proves it." He leaned back, folding his arms over his chest. "And I am plain Mr. de Silva."

His fury changed to fierce protectiveness as he thought of his half sister, at home without any clue of what was happening. "You'll take care of Ana Maria, of course." He knew Thaddeus would have no thought of doing otherwise, but he needed to say it, to retain some measure of agency.

"Of course," Thaddeus said. "But what if I don't want to be the duke?" Thaddeus asked, directing his question to the solicitor. "Can't we just pretend we've never seen these documents? That things are as we always thought?"

Thaddeus was the only person of Sebastian's acquaintance

who had never been envious of Sebastian's position, either as a duke's heir or as the duke himself. Which was why he seemed to have forgotten he was Sebastian's heir. Thaddeus had been actively relieved that he was able to serve in the army, serving Her Majesty rather than his own pleasure.

Whereas Sebastian believed that serving his own pleasure meant that those who relied on him would also benefit. That belief applied mostly to the ladies he pleasured, but he took pains to ensure that his staff and tenants were also taken care of properly.

He was privileged, he knew that, but he used his charm and influence so that everyone would like and appreciate him rather than resent him.

Sebastian was shaking his head before his cousin had finished speaking. "You can't refuse it, Thad. That's the whole point of primogeniture and such. And it would be wrong. It would be a lie. You know that."

Thaddeus's eyes widened. "Primogeniture? Since when do you have such an extensive vocabulary?"

Sebastian shrugged. "Since I might have to *do* something rather than just *be* something." It was a return to his normal insouciant self, but it rang hollow.

Thaddeus's expression drew grim.

"You know, it's not the worst thing in the world to be told you're actually a duke," Sebastian pointed out dryly. Thaddeus glared at him, then folded his arms over his chest.

Poor sad duke.

"So what happens now?" Sebastian asked, directing his question to the solicitor.

The man cleared his throat again, looking unhappy. *Have you also been told everything you thought you were is wrong?* Sebastian thought. *I don't think so. So stop making that expression.*

"Well, the Duke of Hasford—that is—" and he gestured toward Thaddeus "—will assume the position immediately. That will include the estates, the ducal holdings, and everything inherited from the late duke."

Everything, in other words. Sebastian didn't have anything of his own, anything that belonged to—what was his name now?—Sebastian de Silva. His mother's last name. The only thing she had been able to leave him, despite her machinations.

The yawning blank of his future widened in front of him. No money beyond what he had on hand. Likely that belonged to Thad as well. No path forward. No privilege.

"I can't take care of everything right away," Thaddeus said, obviously trying to keep his tone measured. And failing spectacularly. "I command a regiment, it will take time to extricate myself." He sounded desperate. "You can continue for the time being, can't you?" he asked Sebastian.

The solicitor's lips pursed. "That—" he began, before Sebastian interrupted.

"No, Thad." He spoke in a decisive tone. "Much as I would love to help you out by overseeing one of the wealthiest titles in England," he said understatedly, "I cannot." He pointed at the documents. "Those say I cannot. What would it look like if you refused to do your duty? Even for a short time?" He shook his head as he leaned forward. "It would be devastating. The one thing I know in this world is that the Duke of Hasford has responsibilities to the title, to the land, to the tenants and workers, to the country. I've been indoctrinated with that duty since I was born. I cannot betray it." He spoke with the ferocity he normally reserved for flattering a particularly beautiful woman.

Thaddeus clamped his mouth shut, and Sebastian saw a muscle tic in his jaw. That's when he knew Thad wouldn't argue. It was his tell, and Sebastian had taken advantage of it over many card games. But this was one situation where Thad had the winning hand—even though he did not want it.

Sebastian slid the documents back toward the solicitor as he rose out of his chair. Feeling his jaw clench. "I will leave you and the Duke of Hasford to continue your discussion. I presume there is nothing further?" His tone made it clear it would be a presumption if there was.

The solicitor shook his head. "Thank you for coming, Your—that is, Mr. de Silva."

He suppressed a wince at his name. He'd have to grow accustomed to it.

He addressed Thad, noting his cousin's severe expression. Once again, the cousins were in perfect agreement. "I'll vacate the town house as soon as possible, Your Grace. I was planning to launch Ana Maria into Society, so you'll have to take that over. She deserves it."

Whatever happened, at least he knew Ana Maria would be secure. Even if she was also devastated by the turn of events. "I will be available to answer any questions you have regarding the estate management and the tenants and such."

"Seb, you don't have to go right away." Thaddeus looked even grimmer. "This is a lot to absorb, and we'll both need some time to adjust."

Sebastian bit back whatever angry words he wanted to say—it wasn't Thad's fault that Seb's mother had lied. Thad didn't want the title just as much as Seb did. "I'll find somewhere else to go. You'll have to decide if you want to keep the staff. My valet, Hodgkins, will take this hard. If you don't have anyone yet for that position, I'd recommend keeping him on."

The change didn't just mean change for him—it would alter his entire household. His valet, his secretary, the butler, the housekeeper. He had spent six months learning about these people now that he was their master, working with them, assuring them that he was not his careless father. And definitely not his demanding mother. Something he had been thwarted in doing until he had assumed the title. But now the title wasn't his after all.

He wanted to punch something, someone, but that wouldn't do anything but make his knuckles sore.

"Of course. You can trust me to do what's right."

Sebastian wished he were calm enough to sit back down and review the details of the staff with Thaddeus, try to persuade him to give all of them a chance, even though Thad was rightfully proud of his ability to make a quick, decisive decision. And even though some of the staff was still a work in progress—progress Sebastian had been making, with Ana Maria's guidance.

But he couldn't spend another minute here, not without unleashing his anger, and nobody here deserved that.

"I'll see you later, cousin."

He spun on his heel and walked out of the solicitor's office, ignoring Thaddeus calling his name, nodding at the clerks who were working outside. Maintaining his ducal facade even as his world was crumbling around him.

Hours later, Sebastian was exhausted, hungry, and thirsty. He'd spent the time since leaving the solicitor's office pacing through the streets of London, his mind obsessively churning the information over and over again, as though that would change the outcome. Finally, unable to walk any longer, he returned home. As though home was his home.

He didn't have a home anymore. He didn't own anything anymore.

He wasn't who he'd thought he was anymore.

He'd never truly appreciated the Duke of Hasford's town house until it wasn't his any longer, but as he approached the house he viewed it as others did. The most opulent house on the street, it had over two dozen windows in the front alone, enormous pillars serving no apparent purpose beyond declaring that the owner of the house had so much money he could spend it on useless pieces of marble.

It was elegant and extravagant and shameless.

Rather like him, he thought remorsefully. And like the pillars, he was just as useless. Not even propping up the aristocracy.

"Welcome home, Your Grace." His butler, Fletchfield, hesitated for the slightest fraction before saying his honorific. Meaning the news had already spread here, at least to his butler. No doubt it had already spread through most of Society; that a duke could be de-duked, as it were, would be a scandal for the ages.

"Thank you, Fletchfield." Sebastian gave his hat and coat to the butler. "Whiskey in my office. I'll be down after I change."

"Yes, Your . . ." But the butler's words were lost as Sebastian sprinted up the stairs to his bedroom, turning the knob and flinging the door open.

His valet, Hodgkins, was there, treating him as he usually did. So the news likely hadn't reached beyond Fletchfield. It would, of course, and Sebastian wished he could assure them, all of them, that they would be fine even if he wasn't, but he couldn't make that guarantee, even though he knew Thaddeus would do the right thing. They'd be fearful of losing their positions no matter what—his mother had terrorized them enough during her tenure.

"I'll be changing to go out," he said.

Go out where? a voice asked.

Damned if I know.

He glanced around the room as Hodgkins bustled about, getting his things. He hadn't gotten around to redecorating the master bedroom after his parents died, and everything was done in his mother's style, discreetly tasteful colors indicating just how very expensive it was. The only thing in the room that was truly his was his shaving kit, which his father had gifted to him on his sixteenth birthday. It was engraved with his initials, although they weren't *his* initials any longer, were they?

But it was his, even if nothing else was.

Soon Sebastian was rigged out in his most ostentatious clothing—a gold patterned waistcoat, an elegant black necktie, slim trousers, and a blindingly white shirt—even though he had no place to be. He considered attending a party or five—there were plenty of invitations—but they were all addressed to the Duke of Hasford. Not Mr. Sebastian de Silva.

And he knew that the party guests, those of whom liked to gossip, which meant most of them, would take no time in reminding him he was a mere mister now.

"Damn it," he said to himself as he descended the stairs. He took a quick left into his office, where he spotted the tray with the whiskey right away. "Thank God," he murmured, pouring himself a healthy amount. He'd been spending a lot of time in this room, learning the estate affairs, taking meetings with the staff. Once he'd inherited the title from his father, it had felt crucial that he focus on his responsibilities rather than his pleasure.

He could return to pleasure now. But he didn't want to. Nor would he have the privilege of doing so—he'd have to . . . *work* for his living now?

He'd never considered that possibility when he'd contemplated his future.

The enormity of the change hit him all over again. Nothing was his. Not his clothing, not this house, not anything. Not even the name he'd grown up with. He was Mr. Sebastian de Silva now. Nothing more.

He really needed whiskey, even though that wasn't his either. He knew, however, that Thaddeus wouldn't begrudge him a stiff drink.

He held the glass up to his mouth, then frowned as he spotted the signet ring on his right pinkie.

The signet ring that had belonged to his father, the Duke of Hasford. That was passed on to all the dukes in succession.

He put the glass back down on the table, yanked the ring from his finger, and flung it into the corner of the room.

"Your aim is improving."

Sebastian heard Nash's voice before he saw him. His friend was standing in the shadows, as usual, but emerged into the light, holding the ring, his usual grim smile on his lips.

Nash stood as tall as Sebastian, but where Sebastian was lean and elegant, Nash, the Duke of Malvern, was pure force. He looked more like a stevedore than a duke, and he behaved more like one as well, preferring the company of common men to his literal peers.

He'd grown up with Sebastian and Thaddeus, and the three had maintained their close friendship through inheritance, the army, romantic heartbreak, and feckless parents.

"You've heard." Sebastian picked his glass up and drained it as Nash approached.

He poured a glass and handed it to Nash, who took it and drank it all down, barely wincing at the burn of the whiskey.

"I did." Nash held his glass out for more. "I thought that between you and Thad, you might need me more."

Sebastian snorted as he poured more liquid into Nash's glass. "I'm not certain about that. Thaddeus looked as though someone had deliberately disorganized his papers when we heard the news." He glanced reflexively at the surface of his desk, which was neatly arranged. He hoped his secretary would meet Thad's exacting standards.

Nash chuckled. "What are you going to do?"

That was the question of the day, wasn't it? "I don't know." Sebastian sat down on the sofa, leaning his head back and closing his eyes. "I need to tell Ana Maria. I need to let the staff know, although I suspect the news has already reached them. But first I need to—"

"Get drunk," Nash supplied. "With me at a place where you won't run into as many of those condescending pricks."

"Which condescending pricks?" He waved a hand as Nash opened his mouth. "Never mind, I know you mean all of them. Tell me how you really feel," Sebastian replied dryly. He sat up, slapping his hands on his thighs. "Your idea is a good one, but I can't get too drunk because I need to speak with my sister tomorrow."

Thank goodness Ana Maria was out this evening. He didn't remember where she had gone, but there was no danger Ana Maria would get in any kind of trouble—his half sister was remarkably staid in her behavior, given how wild her younger half brother was. Or had been, until he'd inherited six months ago.

"Drunk enough to take the edge off then," Nash said. "Miss Ivy's, I think. It's new."

"As long as there is an abundance of whiskey and a paucity of condescending pricks," Seb replied.

About the Author

MEGAN FRAMPTON writes historical romance under her own name and romantic women's fiction under the name Megan Caldwell. She likes the color black, gin, dark-haired British men, and huge earrings, not in that order. She lives in Brooklyn, New York, with her husband and son.

meganframpton.com

meganframptonbooks meganf